# Acclaim

"*Once Upon A Christmas Past* is *A Christmas Carol* meets Jane Austen's *Emma*, complete with all the beauty of a Victorian London Christmas and match-making ghosts! Fast-paced, full of intrigue and swoony romance, I could not put this book down, yet was sad when it was over. A wonderful companion novel to *Olivia Twist*, and a perfect addition to the world of Dickens that embodies the spirit(s) of Christmas."

—CAREY CORP, author of *Shades of Neverland*

"I am convinced this is the most perfect Christmas book to have ever been written. It not only hits every necessary trope but brings each one to new heights. Every page sparkles with the hope, joy, and magic of Christmas. An enchanting companion to *A Christmas Carol* that Charles Dickens himself would have been thoroughly delighted by. I didn't want it to end."

—CHELSEA BOBULSKI, author of the All I Want for Christmas series

"This is one of the best holiday stories I've ever read! The magic of the holiday season, the poignancy of rags to riches, the unexpected, the ghosts, and the perfect amount of swoon all make this a must-read for anyone who is looking for their next cozy adventure between the pages of a book."

—APRIL J. SKELLY, author of *Murder at Mistlethwaite Manor* and *A Lethal Engagement*

# Once Upon a Christmas Past

# Once Upon a Christmas Past

Quill & Flame
PUBLISHING HOUSE

## LORIE LANGDON

**Quill & Flame**
PUBLISHING HOUSE

*Once Upon A Christmas Past*

Copyright ©2024 by Lorie Moeggenberg

Published by Quill & Flame Publishing House, an imprint of Book Bash Media, LLC.

www.quillandflame.com

All rights reserved.

No part of this publication may be reproduced, digitally, stored, or transmitted in any form without written permission from the publisher, except as permitted by U.S. copyright law.

This is a work of fiction. Names, characters, and incidents are products of the author's imagination or are used ficticiously. Any similarity to actual people, living or dead, organizations, business establishments, and/or events is purely coincidental.

NO AI TRAINING: Without any limitation on the author or Quill & Flame's exclusive copyright rights, any use of this publication to train generative artificial intelligence is expressly prohibited.

Cover design by AJ Skelly, Typography by EAHCreative

www.ajskelly.com

www.eahcreative.com

# Chapter One

*S*now drifted up like smoke under tattered boots as the boy ran. Master Scrooge would have his hide if he were one minute late with the hoary man's stew. The boy glanced up at the ancient church tower, its spire invisible in the swirling clouds of fog, and dared the gruff old bell not to mark the hour. But even as he pushed his legs faster past shop windows brightened with holly sprigs and scarlet berries, a tremendous vibration rang through the icy air like teeth chattering in a frozen head.

*The bell tolled...*

**1864**

**The outskirts of London, Hill Orphanage**

"To begin, your father is dead. There is no doubt whatever about that." The solicitor pushed wire-rimmed glasses up the slope of his hawkish nose. "The cause of death is inconclusive, but he's dead, to be sure." Mr. Veck moved on to the next paper as if the words he'd uttered hadn't sent a battering ram through Brit's chest. "I have the register of his burial here, signed by a clergyman, his clerk, the undertaker..."

The wind blew raw and keen, penetrating to the very bones. Brit suppressed a shiver and glanced out the set of long windows overlooking the garden where winter battled against autumn to make its presence known.

Brit had asked his employers, Jack and Olivia MacCarron, not to search for his parents, or anyone's family, for that matter. They were orphans for a reason; namely their parents were addicts, criminals, vagrants, insane, or as Mr. Veck had so astutely pointed out, dead. Why dredge up past pain?

To date, only one child, a girl of autumnal curls who Ms. Olivia had taken in three years past, had been happily reunited with a mother who worked as a kitchen maid in a decent household. The girl's father had sold her to pay a debt without the mother's knowledge.

"...John and George Griffin, the executor, the coroner, the magi—"

"That's quite enough, Veck." Jack MacCarron, Brit's mentor, and owner of the orphanage raised a palm. "Get to the point."

The little man lowered his spectacles, gray eyes dancing as his dark brows rose into his wrinkled forehead. "I certainly did not mean to offend. However, the father's death must be distinctly understood as it pertains to the son's inheritance. So you see, there is a method to my madness, Mr. MacCarron."

"Let's get straight to the method then, eh?" Jack's tone had frozen the blood in many a man.

"Right." The attorney's Adam's apple bobbed as he assessed his paperwork. "Then allow me to dispense with a certain formality.

Brit, do you have any distinguishing features, such as scars, birthmarks, or the like?"

Brit didn't have to think long. He lifted the leg of his trousers to show a jagged scar indenting the muscle of his calf, the origins of which he did not recall.

Mr. Veck grinned. "Thank you, sir. This confirms your identity, although I didn't need it considering you are the male personification of your mother and have the imposing physical presence of your father. But for legal purposes I had to make the confirmation."

"You knew my parents?"

"Oh, yes, I've worked for the family since before you were born. Now then, for the establishment of Bartholomew's—"

"I don't...recognize that name. I prefer Brit Crane." Brit crossed his arms over his chest, not appreciating the solicitor's presence. After so many years of hardship, Brit had a good life. He'd learned mathematics, science, and literature, and thanks to the indomitable Mrs. March, he possessed the manners of a gentleman—when he chose to use them. Now, at ten and eight, he taught literature and helped run the orphanage. He'd found a purpose and a family. Learning his birth name was *Bartholomew Whitney Rhys Griffin* didn't mean a wit.

Mr. Veck glanced between Brit and Jack, the newly lit fire cracking and smoking as if in response to their impatience. After a prolonged moment, the solicitor sat straighter in his chair and bobbed his head in a kind of seated bow. "Brit Crane is a fine name. However, by all social tenets, I should be addressing you by your title."

Brit's scalp tingled as the blood drained from his head, but before he could contemplate the man's meaning, he landed another blow.

"In precise fact, your entitlement." Only appearing the tiniest bit smug, Mr. Veck stated, "Your father, Whitney Rhys Griffin was the esteemed and extremely wealthy, Earl of Wexford."

Brit froze like a pickpocket caught by the wrist. The ability to speak, move, or even breathe had left him. This chap was surely mistaken. Brit didn't remember his family. Only the moment he'd watched a blasted surgeon bleed his mother to death. At which point, he must have been a toddler in nappies because the rest of his childhood had grown sketchy. He recalled snippets of crying inconsolably as a dark-skinned woman in colorful skirts picked him up, and then nothing until Ebenezer Scrooge had hired him as his house boy, only to boot him out a few weeks later.

That's when he'd begun living on the streets, stealing to survive.

Warmth enveloped his left hand, which had locked onto the arm of the chair in a death grip, and Brit glanced over to find Jack's fingers squeezing his in reassurance. This man, for all intents and purposes, was his father. Not some bloody earl he'd never known.

Finally finding his voice, he barked. "Are you deranged? I'm a street kid. *A tooler.*"

"That may be," Mr. Veck said. "Your living relations claim you were kidnapped at five years of age."

Brit swallowed hard. "My living relations?"

"Yes, you have two brothers." Mr. Veck shuffled through his papers and peered through the lower part of his spectacles. "John and George, sons from your mother's first marriage. It says here that her first husband died shortly after the boys were born. Following your mother and father's marriage, the brothers were legally adopted by the earl."

"I don't understand." Brit turned to Jack and then back to the solicitor. "What does all of this mean?"

"That you are an earl, and a terribly wealthy one, Lord Wexford."

Brit stared at Mr. Veck. He wanted to insist that he was not Lord Wexford, just plain Brit Crane, the boy who'd chosen his surname from a fiction book. Brit the orphan. Brit the crook turned English teacher. Instead, he looked to Jack for guidance, but the man appeared as flummoxed as himself.

Jack blinked twice before snapping out of his shock. "How wealthy, exactly?"

The attorney shuffled through his papers again. "The bequeath includes the country seat, Wexford Manor in Hampshire and its some two hundred acres, the Mayfair townhome, railway shares, English funds, stocks, silver plate, of course, and a vault of gold coin…"

"In total, sir," Jack interrupted. "In total, what will Brit inherit?"

"Well, that will depend…there is one…" His gaze ferreted between Jack and Brit. "…er…one stipulation that will dictate whether Lord Wexford retains his inheritance."

"Elaborate." Jack gripped the arms of his chair and leaned forward.

The solicitor spoke quickly. "As part of the entail, the will states a quite specific condition. For Lord Wexford to claim his title and fortune, he must find a wife before he turns twenty years of age. This Christmas day, 1864, to be precise."

Brit slumped back in his seat and pinched the bridge of his nose, unsure if any of this could be real. *Brothers. Estates. Marriage. An earldom.* Wouldn't he remember if he'd been born into a noble family of wealth and privilege?

And if it were true, how did he go from a spoilt toff to picking pockets to survive?

None of it made sense.

Even the man's dates were all wrong. "I have two more years before I turn twenty."

When Mr. Veck did not respond, Brit lowered his hand to see the man pushing a paper across the table. A certificate, stating his date and time of birth as December 25th, 1845, five in the morning. He had turned nineteen this Christmas past.

"Why?" Brit managed to croak.

The attorney removed his spectacles and sat them on his knee. "Assuming you do not mean your date of birth…"

Jack made a noise close to a growl and the man rushed on.

"The stipulation of marriage is most often included to ensure an heir is produced and the title and lands stay in the family line."

A streak of lightning flashed outside the window followed shortly by thunder and then another flash. Brit turned to stare as shadows thrust themselves into the room. The boom that followed rattled the glass and drew a shriek from one of the children. Feet pounded overhead as, Brit presumed, the kids ran to the windows. A true thunderstorm was a rare occurrence in London.

A blaze, like full summer sun, lit the windows, tailed by an explosion that rumbled through the very floorboards, followed by cheers and whoops sounding from above stairs as if God himself had created a firework display for the children's delight. At the next flicker, the distinct sound of Chip Lightheart's voice began to count, and the other kids joined in. "One! Two! Three..."—*BOOM!* Their carefree laughter, safe and sound inside a home where they had plenty of warm food, cozy beds, friendship, and love, settled hard in Brit's chest.

He faced Mr. Veck. "I don't want it."

The lawyer poised with a glass of ink in one hand and a sleek, black pen in the other. "Pardon?"

"Not the money, the title, the lands...I have everything I could ever need." He turned to Jack. "I appreciate what you've done, finding my family and all, but I do not wish..." A grumble of thunder interrupted him and when he spoke again his voice had gone raw. "I don't wish for anything to change."

"Change is necessary for growth," Ms. Olivia spoke as she glided into the room, her sleeping baby girl snuggled on her shoulder. Brit had to assume she'd heard a good portion of what he wished to turn down. She had a way of knowing just about everything that went on at Hill House.

Lightning flared, and the baby squirmed, letting out a tiny cry.

"Jack, can you take Franny, please?"

"Always." Jack reached out, the child doll-like in his large hands as he tucked the soft bundle into the crook of his arm and gazed at his daughter's face. Brit never tired of the wonder that transformed the former street lord's expression at the sight of his baby girl. With her mother's dark-gold curls and Jack's clear blue eyes, she was a beauty at less than a year old.

Baby Franny popped a thumb into her mouth and dark lashes fell to plump cheeks. Olivia placed a hand on Jack's shoulder.

"I believe she's ready for her nap, dear." She nodded toward the attorney. "I can take it from here."

Jack stood and walked to the door but paused and turned back around. "You'll make the right choice, Brit." He grinned, his brows lifting. "Unlike me, you always do."

As the last rumbles of thunder faded, Olivia sat in the chair Jack had vacated, fluffed her heavy silk skirts, and straightened her spine. "Mr. Veck, we are going to need a private moment. You can await us in the parlor."

Summarily dismissed, the man stuffed his ink and pen back into its case, gathered his loose papers and stood. "As you say, Mrs. MacCarron." With a quick bob, he exited and shut the door behind him.

Olivia leaned over and took one of Brit's large ruddy hands in her delicate white fingers. "Do you remember when I found you on the waterfront?"

"Aye, I remember."

"Do you recall the first thing I said to you?"

He gave a slow nod. "You said, 'I'll never take anything from you.'"

"That is still true, Brit. I would never rob you of something so precious. Go find your family, claim your title  and inheritance. Your home will always be here waiting." Her golden eyes filled with tears. "And if you still wish to teach, you can do that too."

Brit stared at the rivers of rain flowing down the windows. He'd grown too comfortable. The kiss of death for an orphan thief. One had to remain vigilant to survive. But as he considered everything he'd learned from Mr. Veck, his instincts—that sixth sense that kept him alive on the streets—fired up once again, humming a warning.

He had two older brothers and a father who had recently passed on. If Jack had so easily uncovered his past, why had his family been unable to locate him? And if he'd truly been kidnapped, what could they possibly have wanted with a toddler?

He'd always assumed his dark, wavy hair, brown eyes, and perpetually tan skin meant the old Romani woman who'd sold him to Scrooge had been a relative. Perhaps a cousin his mother had instructed to take him in on the event of her death. But now that didn't make sense.

His past didn't add up.

Brit grinned and squeezed Olivia's hand before releasing it. "You'll let me come back and teach, even if I'm a blasted toff?"

"Especially!" She flashed a dimpled smile. "Can you imagine the publicity a literature-teaching-royal could bring us?"

Laughter erupted from his chest. Olivia had a way of getting him out of his own head. She didn't give a fig about publicity; all their kids were rescued off the streets. "I'm not sure an earl is royalty."

"Well, nobility then." She sobered. "You've always been noble and brilliant and brave…"

"All right, that's enough!" He laughed, his face burning at her praise.

She lifted a brow. "So, you've decided then?

Funny that she realized that before he did himself. With a decisive nod, he replied, "I'm going to meet my brothers and get the answers I need."

"And what of your inheritance?"

"That remains to be seen. But as to finding a wife and marrying by Christmas...not bloody likely."

# Chapter Two

*H*eart rattling in his chest like rusty chains, the boy careened toward a party of scruffy men and boys gathered around a great fire in a brazier. The cold slipped beneath his short trousers and exposed arms poking like sticks from his coat. Flames of rapturous heat reached for him as he passed the blaze.

*The bell tolled two...*

"Raven Cratchit, get your nose out of that book this instant!"

Raven jumped at the screech of her mother's voice but continued reading until the book was jerked from her hands and slammed shut. "Well, I suppose I'm finished."

Mrs. Cratchit, a handsome woman with salt and pepper hair and a pleasantly plump figure, had never been one for dawdling when there was a social engagement to attend. And let there be no doubt, her mother saw Raven's absorption with *An Introduction to the Study of Experimental Medicine* as procrastination of the worst sort—and she would not be wrong. Raven much preferred her studies to the arduous dinner that lay ahead.

Mother dropped the massive text on the bureau with a thud and then scooped Raven's velvet gown off the bed. "Where is Mary? That maid will be the death of me yet!"

Raven rose from her bedroom window seat and stretched her arms to the ceiling with a yawn. "Cook sent Mary to the butcher to collect a ham. The kitchen maid is ill, you know. I took her one of my poultices and a strong peppermint tea, but with her drainage that putrid green, I instructed Mrs. Bowley to keep her out of service for at least a week or risk infecting the household."

Her mother stood hands on hips; the voluminous folds of Raven's sapphire velvet gown looped through her elbow. "A ham?"

"A ham." Out of everything Raven had said, leave it to her mother to focus on the mundane.

"Who ever heard of sending a lady's maid to the butcher?" Mother shook her head in abject disgust. "And on the day of your engagement dinner."

"Yes, that." Raven plopped into a chair, lifted her skirt, and began to roll down a cotton stocking, her mind on a patient she'd seen the day before at Hill House. The child had chronic spasms of the bronchi that made breathing difficult, especially during physical exertion. And the boy never seemed to stop moving. His previous physician believed the asthmatic condition to be psychosomatic and advised his guardians to treat him for mental depression.

Raven lifted her arms and allowed her mother to remove the day dress over her head.

After spending less than five minutes with Chip Lightheart, Raven had known the boy's diagnosis to be incorrect. Chip certainly suffered from bronchi asthma, but he did not display a bit of melancholy.

She stood and sucked in her breath as her mother cinched her corset.

Her earlier study of Claude Bernard's theories on investigational medicine gave her an idea… "Oh!" She'd not taken a full step toward her bookcase when Mama yanked her back by the laces.

"I'll get you into this gown if it kills me, young lady." Her mother tugged with unnecessary force.

"But mama, I've just had an epiphany. Chip has spasmodic contractions in his lungs that are unresponsive to conventional treatments…" Her words trailed off at the possibilities and then picked up again. "The Chinese use acupuncture…I need Peter's text. And I believe he has a needle kit—"

"Darling," Mother sighed. "I do admire how you wish to help others, but as we speak, your brother is preparing for *your* engagement dinner. You may talk to him all you like about lung spasms and Asian remedies in the carriage." Taking Raven by the shoulders, Mrs. Cratchit turned her around and began adjusting her sleeves and bodice. "But please promise me, on figgy pudding and all you hold dear, that you will not discuss medicine at the Griffins' home."

Raven lifted an amused brow. "On figgy pudding?"

Her mother glanced up from fussing with the sapphire silk bows at Raven's elbows, mirth sparkling in her eyes. "I know how you adore Christmas. Perhaps even a bit more than doctoring?"

"I'd say they are neck and neck in the race for my affections."

Mrs. Cratchit straightened. "And where does Jonathan Griffin place in this hypothetical race?"

A knock sounded on the bedroom door, saving Raven in the nick of time from admitting her betrothed lagged somewhere near the back of the race.

Mrs. Cratchit opened the door to the parlor maid who held a brown paper parcel in her hands. "A delivery for Miss Cratchit."

Mother took the package and before the door could be shut behind the maid, Belinda swept into the room, exclaiming rapturously, "It's from Cadbury Brothers!"

Belinda, two years Raven's senior, was her elder sister and closest confidant. But not even Belinda knew of her struggles to feel something—*anything*—for the man who'd asked her to spend forever with him. John's support of her doctoral pursuits compelled a shallow sort of affection towards him. But neither of them had spoken of love.

"Open it, Rav, before I do so myself!" Belinda urged.

Raven ripped through the paper to find a stationary card signed, "With affection, John Griffin." And a box that smelled like heaven on a stick. Or in a bar, to be precise. Nestled inside the tissue paper were five glistening chocolate blocks. Her mouth watered at the sugary cocoa scent as she snapped off a piece and placed it on her tongue.

As the confection melted on Raven's tongue, her eyes rolled back in her head and she groaned, her sentiments toward John Griffin sprinting into the race. The man sure knew how to give a gift. Last week it had been princess-cut sapphire earbobs. The week before, a tiny Persian kitten. Which, although quite adorable, she had re-gifted to her maid, Mary. Between Raven's medical studies at the Florence Nightingale School and patient rounds with her brother, she simply did not have time to care for the sweet, little creature.

She popped another morsel into her mouth and savoring the rich, heavenly bite, spun on her toes in a tight circle. "You can never have too many books or too much chocolate, I say!"

"Oh, please!" Mrs. Cratchit chided. "Raven, you're going to stain your dress. Can you please take this seriously?"

"I take many things seriously, Mother, but chocolate is not one of them."

"What about *Joohhnn*?" Belinda teased.

Mirroring Belinda, Mother asked, "Do you take your engage-ment seriously?"

Raven slumped on the bed, mid-twirl, and dropped the last square of chocolate back into the box.

"Do you not love him, then?" Her mother asked softly.

Raven sighed. "I love how supportive John is, and how well respected he is in the community, which will open countless doors for me as a female physician. He's nice and funny and attentive..."

"But..."

"But he doesn't raise my body temperature."

"Raven Anne Cratchit!" Her mother's scandalized tone was likely to alert the Widow Snyder two blocks down.

"Does he not make your heart go pitter-patter?" Belinda ques-tioned with a sad sort of longing. Bel's fiancé, whom she'd loved with deep passion, had cheated on her with a Baroness. Bel had nullified their engagement, subsequently ruining her reputation. Well, it had not been the nullification exactly, but the pot of tepid tea that she'd dumped on the Baroness's elaborately festooned head in the middle of the Dodson's soiree that had caused a blazing scandal. Bel had never recovered, socially or otherwise.

"Sadly, my heart does not go pitter-patter," Raven confirmed.

Her mother harrumphed.

"Elliot used to make my hair stand on end when he touched me. He may have been a cad, but when we kissed…" Bel's voice trailed off as she wiggled her brows.

Raven turned to her mother. "Sorry Mama, but it's true. I've studied the body's physical responses to attraction. Elevated heart rate, dilated pupils, sweaty palms, heated neck and cheeks, rapid blood flow to…"

"Oh, sweet Lord!" Mother fanned her scarlet cheeks with her hand. "How have I raised such a heathen?"

Raven met Belinda's gaze and they broke out in hysterical giggles.

After Raven's laughter dissipated, Mrs. Cratchit sat next to her and squeezed her daughter's shoulders. "But he is a good man, dear."

"And handsome," Belinda added.

"You will grow to love him, I'm quite sure," Mother asserted.

"And when he sees the way that royal blue gown matches your eyes, he's going to profess his undying love!" Bel pronounced as she drifted toward Raven's abandoned candy square.

"His love for chocolate, perhaps," Raven muttered and snatched the sweet before her sister could reach it.

Bel's protest was interrupted by another knock at the door. This one sharp and urgent.

"Come in!" Raven called.

Mr. Holt, the family butler, rushed inside waving a letter. "Miss Raven, there's an emergency at Hill House. One of the children is gravely ill!"

She shot to her feet. "Is it young Chip?"

Mrs. Cratchit stepped in front of her daughter and addressed the servant. "What of Peter?"

"He was called to St. Bart's less than an hour past." Mr. Holt handed Raven the missive. "Some sort of carriage accident with multiple injuries."

Skimming the note, Raven found it was as she suspected; Chip had gone into full respiratory distress.  With no time to lose, she raced to the bookcase, dictating orders. "Mother, run to Peter's room and get his acupuncture kit. Mr. Holt, have the phaeton brought 'round..." The two-seater would make better time than the closed carriage.

"But the engagement party is in less than an hour!" her mother unnecessarily pointed out. "Surely, there's another doctor who can help."

Locating the Chinese medicine volume on the shelf, Raven found the correct chapter, shoved the letter in to mark the page and ran to the dressing room for her shoes. She'd never attempted acupuncture. But the book had a step-by-step process, including a diagram. She would have to study the procedure on the way. Adrenaline pumped through her veins, sharpening her mind, and clearing her emotions as she grabbed her instrument bag.

"What will I tell the Griffins?" Her mother blocked her path to the door.

"Tell them I'm going to save a boy's life. Dinner will have to wait."

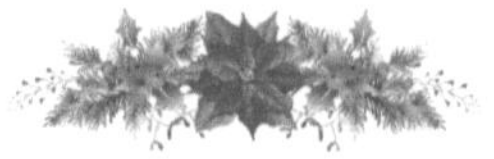

Christmastime in London was Brit's least favorite time of year. He stared out the carriage window as they passed a holiday market with evergreen-wreathed booths, merchants selling hand-sewn dollies with pastel cotton skirts, stuffed bears wearing bowties, and wooden trains painted in bright red and green. One vendor claimed to sell the best hot chocolate in the city, while another hawked baskets piled high with sunny oranges, fat plums, and scarlet apples, each handle tied with a festive bow. Just beyond the bustling marketplace, ice skaters wrapped snug and warm in mufflers and fur-lined jackets glided across a frozen pond; some holding hands, others wobbling along while a young group of boys zipped around them chasing a puck. Their cheers and laughter reached all the way into the carriage.

Brit turned away.

Christmases at Hill Orphanage were merry enough with the orphans decorating multiple trees, exchanging handmade gifts, and partaking in a feast that left them all lulling about like stuffed pigs. But Brit's memories never allowed him to fully enjoy the holiday. Those lean years when he'd felt responsible for his ragtag group who stole to survive haunted him. There was no sipping mugs of spiced cider or munching on sugar biscuits while presents were handed out in front of the fire. They had been lucky to survive another day.

Never mind that many of those boys were safe and healthy at Hill House now. Some of them weren't sheltered and never would be again.

The carriage jerked to a stop in front of a house that towered four stories above him. He jumped down to the walk on his own, asked the driver to wait, and stared up at the pristine, white bricks and multitude of glittering windows. Columns on either side of the wide front door supported a portico topped with elaborate stone crenelations and a statue of a winged creature with a lion's head—a griffin.

Brit's gut hardened at the reminder of an identity he could not claim. A name he did not want. The reading of the will and his sudden knowledge of family and wealth beyond his imagining did not feel real. In fact, his pulse hammered as if a copper might jump out from behind the hedge and arrest him for the tooler he was!

His hands clenched into fists at his sides, and he forced one foot in front of the other until he reached the door and banged a polished brass knocker.

A staunch-looking butler took his card and ushered Brit into a black and white tiled foyer that soared several stories overhead, and a grand staircase curved up to a second-floor gallery. Brit had heard of such extravagance but had never witnessed it with his own eyes.

He turned toward a set of open doors and spotted a man seated behind a large walnut desk. A man he assumed was John Griffin, *his half brother*.

Brit watched John Griffin's face over the butler's head. He reserved the right to skepticism as he analyzed the man; broad shoulders hunched, short-cropped dark hair, forehead wrinkled in concentration, wide jaw set in a firm line.

"Lord Wexford," the butler's voice sounded strained. "There is a Mr....Crane here to see you."

When John lifted his head, his eyes grew wide, and he shot to his feet. Brit moved from behind the butler and noted that his brother's height could compete with Brit's own, which was formidable.

John's gaze narrowed and then widened in wonder. "Bart?"

"Brit," he corrected as he clutched the roll of parchment in his hand, proof of his new identity, and widened his stance. Unsure if he should act the bludger or the toff, Brit crossed his arms in front of his chest. Then, deciding the man was no physical threat, he uncrossed them again. "A Mr. Veck has recently informed me that my birthname was Bartholomew Griffin, but I prefer Brit Crane."

His brother stood in front of the desk, hands at his sides, jaw unhinged. He had light eyes, the color of a cloudy sky. A paunch protruded over his trousers, unlike Brit's flat stomach. He couldn't say if his own athletic build was more due to all those years of starvation or the endless cricket matches he played at Hill House. But John appeared extremely well-fed. Soft. Indulged.

A dark emotion burned in Brit's chest that he promptly squashed as he searched John's face for some defining characteristic, something other than their similar dark hair and height that identified them as relation. And then John Griffin smiled, long dimples bracketing both sides of his wide mouth; a smile Brit knew well.

John rushed forward and enclosed Brit in a bear hug that nearly lifted his feet off the floor. "When Mr. Veck told us he thought he'd found you, I confess, I did not believe it. But now looking at you...after all these years..."

"George!" John bellowed as he released Brit.

A bit off balance, Brit stepped back and turned to find a shorter, narrower version of John rushing into the room.

George moved towards Brit, eyes shining. "There have been false hopes in the past, but...*you* couldn't be anyone other than our brother, the boy who looks just like our dear departed mother."

George extended his hand and Brit shook it, all the while, gritting his teeth against the monster that roared inside him, demanding answers. Instead, he worked hard to maintain the civil façade Mrs. March had drilled into his head at every opportunity.

"A pleasure, gentlemen." Brit watched a maid slowly pass the doorway, then another, followed by an older woman who didn't hide her curious stare. "Is there someplace we may converse in private?"

"Of course, I'll close the doors, my lord," George said with a bow.

"I'm not your *lord*," Brit snapped. "I'm not anyone's blasted—" He cut himself off and sank into a chair before his cockney accent reared its ugly head. Or worse, he clouted one of his newly discovered brothers in the face—a long-buried defense mechanism from his years living in the ghettos. When in doubt, punch and ask questions later.

"I believe a spot of tea is in order," John said. "And perhaps a bit of..."

The conversation between John and George continued in hushed tones, but Brit was no longer listening. It had just occurred to him that the four-story Mayfair townhome with its plush carpets, gilt-papered walls, and even the silk-upholstered chair he sat upon, belonged to him—

Brit the street rat with no last name who hadn't owned more than a wardrobe of modest clothing and a few books his entire life.

Brit squeezed his temples. This new reality stretched beyond his comprehension, but the bequest had stated unequivocally that every last brick would be his.

According to Veck, there had been an addendum added several years past that left the earldom and all its holdings to John Griffin so long as Brit remained missing. Now that he'd been discovered alive, the second will had become null and void, cutting out his half brothers entirely. Whether he did so or not, depended largely on the answers to the questions swirling in his mind.

"You've arrived at an opportune time, brother," George was saying. "This very evening we're hosting an engagement dinner for John's fiancée's family. You'll stay, of course."

Brit gave a noncommittal nod, noting the timeliness of his brother's engagement. If Brit did not marry by his coming birthday, John's marriage would solidify his claim to the earldom.

As soon as the tea and cakes were brought in and the doors closed, Brit asked the two men sitting across from him, "How did I manage to get myself kidnapped?"

John met his gaze. "A man of direct intent, I see. An admirable trait."

"Yes, so get on with it," Brit said levelly.

George sat forward and folded his hands. "Right. Well, we don't have much detail, I'm afraid, as we were children ourselves at the time."

"How old?" Brit asked.

"I was twelve and George was eleven," John replied. "We were both mourning our mother and then when you were taken…" He stared out the front window with a far-off look.

"We could not comprehend that our family was falling apart," George finished.

"What of my father? Did he even try to find me?" Brit questioned.

John's gaze snapped back to his. "He ripped the world apart looking for you. At times, it was as if a demon possessed him. He didn't eat. Didn't sleep. Didn't speak to us except to interrogate us for answers. He may not have been our blood father, but he was the only one we'd ever known, and his disregard confused us. If I would have known—" He cut himself off and crossed his arms before continuing, "Father hired a private investigator, and they combed the countryside together. We were in Hampshire when you went missing, you see. Lots of open space and ground to cover."

A tiny light sparked in Brit's chest at the thought of his father "ripping the world apart" to find him. But then reality doused the pleasure. There had been no rescue, no joyful reunion of father and son. "When did he die? How?"

John handed Brit a cup of tea, something indefinable shifting in his gaze before he replied, "When snow fell on the Christmas after your disappearance and there was no trace of you, he sank into a deep depression."

"Looking back," George added crossing his thin legs. "We can see his grief for Mother had no time to heal before your disappearance. Seven years passed and he just withered away. The doctor said there wasn't much physically wrong with him. That he simply died of a broken heart."

The wind picked up outside, bare branches beat against the window in a staccato rhythm. *Tap. Tap. Tap.* They lashed like clawed fingers poking at Brit's soul. Could it be that he was not the only victim of this tragedy? Not only had his father suffered immeasurable pain, but the men across from him as well. Or had they been happy to see him go, knowing his disappearance secured their futures? One did not grow up in the slums of London without a healthy dose of skepticism. He turned back to the brothers. "What happened exactly? Where was I when I was taken?"

George's eyes darted to his brother before he questioned, "You really don't recall?"

"I was a dashed toddler, wasn't I?" Brit snapped and gripped his thighs, leaning forward. "I have no memory of our home, either of you, or even my father. Not one recollection to connect myself to the life I presumed to live my first four years."

John took a deep breath and as he let it out, his entire countenance softened. "We liked to play in the garden at Wexford Manor. The pond and surrounding forest were our battlegrounds, our pirate ship, our imaginary world. You tagged along every day until George, and I finally included you in our games."

A flash, no more than a single image, pushed into Brit's mind, of wooden swords, Brit tied with rope, and his brothers insisting that he walk the plank. Brit took a gulp of tea, noting the acidic burn as it went down his throat. "What is this?" He held the cup away.

"Something that relaxes me. I took the liberty of adding a nip to your cup, but I'll pour you another if you prefer to abstain," John replied.

Unable to argue with the need for a bit of calming, Brit stared into the cloudy liquid before taking another sip as John painted a picture of their idyllic life in the country.

"Evenings were spent in the withdrawing room, a warm fire crackling in the hearth, while Mother played the pianoforte or embroidered, Father read the papers, and George and I would play draughts chess. Your favorite pastime was stacking blocks into shapes and towers. Father used to praise your creations and then laugh when you knocked them over. You would growl and stomp 'round until you gained mama's attention and she snatched you up in a hug, declaring you, 'Her sweet little monster.'"

Brit drew in a sharp breath and swallowed a huge mouthful of tea to cover his rising emotion. The image of his mother's deathly pale face was replaced by a glowing smile, a soft cheek pressed against his, and the warm scents of spices and vanilla. Could it be a real memory?

"You remembered something, didn't you?" one of his brothers whispered.

"I can't be certain." Brit lifted his gaze. "Did our mother wear a special scent?"

George's smile appeared affirming and melancholy all at once. "Yes, she imported a unique olive oil soap from her homeland of Greece infused with cardamom, cinnamon, and vanilla."

Brit's eyes stung as he drained the tea from his cup and set it down on the tray, his skin contrasting darkly with the white china. It all made sense now—the reason his ruddy skin and black hair made him stand out from the typical Englishman; his mother had been Greek. He felt adrift. Unsure of his own identity or his place in the world. Was he a teacher? A blasted earl? A Greek scholar. He chuckled to himself.

"My lor—er, Brit?"

He looked up and had to concentrate on George's face as the room seemed to grow and then shrink around him. Perhaps too much truth in one sitting had muddled his brain. "Yes?"

"I asked, where have you been all of this time?"

"I lived with a Romani woman, but I don't remember much of her. Only that when I was old enough to work, she sold me to a merchant by the name of Ebenezer Scrooge." Brit heard his voice growing louder, but he was unable to stop it. "He booted me out and I had to make a way."

"Make a way where?" John's brows drew together.

"The streets. A mag pickpocket, I was," Brit insisted. Why did he feel so odd?

"So, you have lived under reduced circumstances?" John inquired.

"Reduced circumstances?" Brit clutched the arms of his chair. "If that's what you call stealing just to eat and going to bed hungry and cold to the bones, all while sleepin' in the gutter, mind. Just the clothes on me back and a pair of tattered boots two sizes too small that I'd stole off a corpse waitin' at the medical school. Aye, reduced circumstances." Brit sunk back in his chair, all blustered out, barely able to keep his eyes open.

His half brothers stared at him in expectation as if awaiting his next act. That's when he realized he couldn't breathe. Like some enormous bludger sat on his chest. He wheezed, and vomit crawled up his throat. John stood and watched him as one might observe a scientific experiment gone wrong.

Or gone horribly right...

Brit leapt from his seat and slammed into John, pushing him into the wall. "What did you do to me?" he growled. The room spun and John's face slid sideways as he replied, "Not a thing. Mayhap you over-indulged before your arrival?"

Brit threw his weight forward and pressed his forearm into John's windpipe, his *brother's* face turning a satisfying shade of purple. "What did you say?"

The door swung open with a bang. "Lord Wexford, stand down!"

It took several moments for Brit to realize Mr. Veck spoke to him and that John's eyes were rolling back in his head. He stepped away and fell backward, stumbling into George, who took him by the shoulders and steadied him on his feet.

"It was just a dash of Laudanum," John croaked.

Brit blinked a few times until his vision cleared enough to see that John held a small glass bottle, skull and crossbones illustrated on the label. Brit had seen his fair share of the drug. Made from opium, it was used for everything from a cough to a sleep aid, but it was highly addictive, and if taken in excess, deadly. Brit never touched the stuff.

An army of spiders skittered over Brit's skin, and he scratched his arm, then his other arm, and his neck. Sucking in quick, shallow gasps, the realization hit him as the words left his mouth. "You poisoned me."

"No!" John pushed off the wall. "I only added a few drops to your tea."

Brit jerked his arm out of George's grasp and stumbled toward the door. His momentum took him straight into the wall. His heart beating hard now, he recognized the danger, even in his befuddled state. He'd once seen a man overdose on Laudanum. The images of the vagrant's muscles seizing as he had gasped his last breath, foam spewing from his mouth, propelled Brit through the door and into the foyer.

Mr. Veck called his name, but Brit pushed through the doors and out into the wind. Staggering down the walk, he shouted, "Roger!"

The driver jumped down from the carriage and barreled toward him. "Mr. Brit, ye look green! I'll get ye to hospital lickety-split."

"No..." Brit gasped, his vision beginning to dim at the edges as he leaned on the driver. "No bloody...crows. Take me...home." Jack and Olivia would know what to do. He had to get to Hill House.

# Chapter Three

*The boy rounded the corner onto Cornhill and his feet hit ice. His left arm windmilled, but he didn't dare balance with his right for fear of splattering the stew, a mistake that would surely cost his employ. Children laughed and slid on their bottoms all around him, soft white comforters wrapped around toasty necks. The boy fell to his seat and lifted his legs, the warm package tucked against his belly as he slid. Silvery snow smacked his cheeks, pulling a twinkle of a smile from his lips.*

*The bell tolled three...*

Raven placed the hair-thin needle into Chip's skin just beneath his nose, amazed that her hands were steady despite the man hovering over her shoulder. Jack MacCarron's reputation for intimidation had not been exaggerated. But as she positioned the last needle and Chip's breathing began to regulate, Mr. MacCarron's iron façade fell away.

When she'd first arrived at Hill House, Chip's respirations were shallow and erratic, his face beginning to turn blue from lack of oxygen. Still, after the traditional breathing exercises failed, it had taken some persuading before Mr. MacCarron had allowed her to try the unconventional acupuncture therapy. She suspected *Mrs.* MacCarron would've been easier to convince, but she and the baby were out visiting family.

The rumors that swirled around Hill House were numerous and of the epic variety. Mainly, that the founders had grown up in the ghettos of London, stealing to survive; Olivia disguised as a boy and Jack as the infamous street lord, The Artful Dodger. But Raven's favorite tale—one that she hoped in her heart was true—depicted a tragically romantic account of Olivia being arrested and Jack, willing to sacrifice his life to save the girl he loved, confessing to the crime. Rumor had it, that Olivia solved the mystery herself, resulting in Jack's exoneration. The couple had married and started the orphanage shortly thereafter.

"That a boy, Chip. You can beat this thing," Jack encouraged as he took a seat across from her young patient.

Chip let out a soft sigh as the contraction in his chest released. Purple shadows framed his blue eyes, his skin appearing translucent. He sat naked from the waist up, needles sticking from strategic points around his abdomen and up to his eyebrows. A haze of burning lavender oil and cloves enveloped him.

"That's right, Chip, breathe deep," Raven instructed. The vapor of the herbs would help reduce inflammation in the bronchi and further open his passages. Although holistic treatments were not taught at the Florence Nightingale School, nor according to Peter, at the medical academy, ancient healers had been using herbal remedies and acupuncture for centuries.

She placed her fingers on Chip's wrist, sending up a prayer of gratitude that his heart rate had returned to normal. The clock on the mantle struck seven, reminding her that if she wished to make the pudding course of her engagement dinner, she had best hurry.

A red-haired gentleman strode into the room, took one look at Chip's needle-covered torso, and stopped short. "Well! Didn't know pincushions were in fashion this season."

Raven gave a weak laugh, as she watched the miniscule needles quiver with Chip's breath. Mr. MacCarron shot her an odd stare just as a thud sounded from overhead, vibrating the walls themselves, followed by a youthful shriek.

Jack stood and tipped his head in Raven's direction. "If you'll excuse me, Miss Cratchit. Duty calls."

"Of course." She dipped a quick curtsy as another rancorous smash sent Jack half running out the door. With one last affirming glance in Chip's direction, Raven crossed the room to gather her things. Mother would have her drawn and quartered if she didn't arrive at Wexford House within the hour.

"And who might this vision of loveliness be?" The red-haired gentleman appeared at her side. "Mr. Archibald Fox, at your service."

Having forgotten his presence, Raven gave a bit of a start. "Er...nice to make your acquaintance, Mr. Fox."

Auburn brows lowered over odd yellow-green eyes. "And you are?"

Raven coiled her stethoscope around her hand. Perhaps his forward manner had set her on edge, but something about this man felt off. "Miss Raven Cratchit. Physician."

"A physician, you say?"

She nodded and gathered the acupuncture text to her chest.

Mr. Fox tipped his head to her. "You may call me Archie, luv."

Meeting his dancing gaze, Raven was suddenly glad she'd declined Belinda's offer to accompany her. The man before her, with his angular face and irreverent, devil-may-care charm, would've drawn her sister in like a banquet of Turkish delight.

"We've only just met Mr. Fox, that would hardly be appropriate."

Covertly eyeing the book in her arms, Archie gave a rueful grin as he dipped into a bow. "My sincere apologies, Miss Cratchit."

An old woman hobbled, faster than Raven would've believed possible for a human of her advanced age, into the parlor and stopped in front of Chip who sprawled across a divan, eyes at half-mast. "Insufferable, boy! What have you done now?"

Without waiting for an answer, the old woman turned to Raven. "Mrs. Lois March, Miss Cratchit. My gratitude for helping this rascal." Mrs. March sank down on the sofa next to Chip and propped her cane against her knee. Raven's gaze swept across the woman's skirts, longing to examine her legs for rheumatism. She could prescribe a cream of—*no, not this visit*, she reminded herself as she returned to the patient at hand.

"How do you feel, Chip?" She leaned in to remove one of the implements where a dot of crimson welled. She must've implanted it too deeply. Not surprising, given the way his chest had heaved during the administration.

"Much improved, Doc Cratchit." He breathed deeply as the old woman took his hand. "But I don't have to keep these stingers in my skin, do I?"

Raven grinned. She rather liked the sound of 'Doc Cratchit.' "Not long. Only a few more minutes—"

A loud bang from the foyer cut off her words. Never a dull moment at Hill Orphanage, apparently. Even as she thought it, a large man stumbled into the room. Dark waves of hair fell over a strong, pale face, his gaze unfocused, his breathing erratic. He was either ill or knock-down drunk.

Archie pushed off the wall where he'd been leaning. "Corned so early, mate?"

The man's wild eyes scanned the room, landed on Chip, and then zeroed in on the crimson-tipped needle clutched between Raven's fingers. Something akin to a roar escaped his throat as he clenched huge hands into fists and rushed her. "Whot 'ave you done, ye bloody crow?"

Raven sprang to her feet and sidestepped as the man fell against the chair, chest heaving.

"Brit!" Jack MacCarron reappeared and grabbed the man's arm, tugging him back as he lunged after her again. "Miss Cratchit helped Chip through a violent breathing attack. She's a healer."

Archie strode over to the newcomer. "What's happened to you, man?"

Brit itched his arm and then clawed at his neck, covered in red streaks. "My throat...is closing."

"Get the boy a drink, you imbecile!" Mrs. March banged her cane on the floor.

Cautiously, lest the big man attempted another attack, Raven moved closer and noticed he exhaled with a sharp wheeze and swallowed excessively.

"He's having an asthmatic attack, like me," Chip said, just as Raven came to a similar conclusion.

"Lay him down on his back," Raven ordered. "On the sofa."

Mr. MacCarron bolstered the larger man under his arm and helped him lie down.

Raven leaned over Brit and put two fingers to the pulse in his neck. His skin was hot to the touch, his heart rate erratic. "Do you have asthmatic spells often?"

"Never."

"Did you eat or drink anything unusual today?"

Brit's eyes met hers and she noticed they were almost black. "Laudanum." He took a shallow breath. "My brother...put it...in my tea."

"Have you ever taken Laudanum before?"

"Once."

"Did you react to it?"

His gaze darted back and forth, his chest heaving as he nodded. "Yes, but not as...severely." His words sounded thick.

"Open your mouth, please."

He did so, and as she suspected; his tongue had begun to swell. Not good. Adverse reactions to substances had little known treatment. However, she suspected his heightened emotions exacerbated his reaction. Many times, the body followed the mind.

She placed her hand on his shoulder and those fathomless eyes searched her face as she instructed, "Focus on your breathing. Inhale deeply." She demonstrated as much as her corset would allow. "And let the air out slowly." She pursed her lips and blew. Brit followed her rhythm, and after a moment had gained a bit of control.

Raven stood and went to Mr. MacCarron. Uncertain of Jack's relationship to Brit, but sure of his authority, she led him away to the hearth and said, "Brit is having a reaction to the Laudanum. Medically speaking, we cannot be sure why it happens, but some individuals cannot process certain substances and they act like poison to their system. He needs to be bled."

"No!" Her new patient reared up like an angry bear and staggered to his feet. The exertion sent him into respiratory distress again, and his legs gave out, sending him back onto the sofa. Jack rushed over and spoke to Brit in soft, urgent tones.

"He watched his mother bled to death by a physician," Archie said quietly.

She stared at the red-haired man and whispered, "He could die if we don't try it."

"I believe he'd rather take his chances," Archie replied.

Raven turned back and watched the man struggle to draw breath. He did not show fear or even exhibit signs of panic as she had no doubt most would if their airway were closing. Instead, this patient...Brit...sat straight up and wheezed. "I will not...be...bled like...a pig to the...slaughter."

Her own chest tightened in empathy, and not a little bit of desperation. She searched her memory for another solution, wishing desperately she could speak to Peter and tap into his vast medical knowledge. Briefly, she considered sending the driver after him. But as she watched, her patient's skin began to turn a sickly gray. There was no time. Besides, if she wished to become a doctor in her own right, she would need to solve medical crises on her own.

She glanced over at young Chip, still covered in needles, his wide blue eyes wet with tears as he watched Brit struggle on the sofa. And an idea occurred. Perhaps she could use the acupuncture technique. She ran for the text laying open where she'd dropped it on the floor and began to read. Some of the same pressure points she'd triggered on Chip, would open airways regardless of the cause of restriction. But that wouldn't help the inflammation itself. She jerked open her medical bag and began to rummage through until she found a glass jar of stinging nettle. She carried the herb with her to treat joint and muscle pain in the elderly, but in her study of early medicine, she'd read it had also been used as an anti-inflammatory.

Raven turned to instruct Mr. Fox, but he seemed to have vanished. "Mr. MacCarron!" She called the man over. "I need someone to run to the kitchen and make a strong tea with this herb."

Jack MacCarron bellowed, "Thompson!"

An older gentleman with the bearing of a soldier raced into the room. "Sir?"

"Listen to Miss Cratchit and do exactly as she says."

Raven turned to the man. "Place this entire jar of nettles in cheesecloth and steep in a teapot for five minutes." He took it, but his gaze glued to Brit in horror. A deep fear etched lines around his mouth, his eyes glistening. Whoever Brit was to the people in this room, it went beyond casual friendship.

Raven gave the man a push. "We can still save him. Hurry!"

With no idea if her words held any truth, she watched Thompson turn on his heel and run. Mrs. March hovered in silence, her face a white sheet of anxiety. The wind whipped outside, a draft slipping up Raven's skirts. She knew from experience giving the woman a chore would be a kindness. "Mrs. March, can you please stoke up the fire."

"Of course."

"Doc, do you need my needles?" Chip asked.

"Thank you, but I have plenty. You may remove any needles you can reach." Her acupuncture kit tucked under her arm, Raven relit the candle beneath the copper pot of lavender and cloves and carried it over to the table by Brit's head. Wisps of vapor surrounded him as he laid back down, his legs draped haphazardly over the sofa edge. She pulled a chair up beside him and placed her fingers on the pulse in his neck. The beats were faint and too much time passed between his breaths. Opening her kit across her lap, she propped the accompanying text on the table. "Mr. MacCarron, I'm going to have to ask you to remove Mr. Brit's clothing above the waist."

Jack did not hesitate but lifted the younger man by the shoulders and tugged off his coat. Raven leaned forward to unbutton Brit's waistcoat and then his shirt. His dark eyes slit open, his breath a husky rasp. Something flashed behind his gaze, an emotion she couldn't place...but whatever it was made her skin heat like fire.

Furious with her lack of emotional control, she snapped at Jack, "Keep him sitting up, and don't allow him to sink back against the cushions."

He gave a tight nod as Raven reviewed her diagram, selected a needle, and faced the wide expanse of Brit's naked chest. With a deep breath, she took his muscled arm and stretched it out, placing the first needle in the inside crook of the elbow. Feeling they both needed the distraction, she began to talk, softly explaining her actions. "I'm applying hair-thin needles to pressure points linked to functions within your body. This first one opens up the lungs."

His eyes hooded, his breath shallow, he didn't react.

"Breathe, Brit," she urged as she selected her next needle and placed it on the side of his right wrist. "This point is also for optimal lung function."

His skin felt so hot to the touch, she stood and leaned behind him, placing a needle at the top of his spine. "This is called GV14, it reduces fever."

He swayed and Jack carefully steadied him. The pungent vapor of the oils clouded around them as Raven placed several more needles at points along Brit's arms. She sat and consulted her text. Turning back, she watched his chest rise and fall, the rhythm deeper and steadier than before.

A detached part of her mind marveled at the mass of him. They shared the same skeletal system, but his bones and muscles were hard as marble and more than twice the size of her own. She ran her finger along his left collarbone. "The point here will assist with breathing difficulties." He watched the path of her finger. "As well as on the opposite side."

After placing a few more needles along his upper chest, she asked, "How are you feeling now?"

After a moment of his eyes roaming over her face, his gaze met hers and locked in. "Dizzy. You appear to have four...startlingly blue eyes."

Her heart stopped for a moment. "Did you say four?" Although his breathing had begun to regulate, the mental issue could indicate a continued lack of oxygen. She lifted her hand. "How many fingers am I holding up?"

He tried to focus but then closed his eyes, a half-smile tilting his mouth. "That would depend on...how many arms...you have."

Brit swayed and Jack gripped his shoulders, his face tight with worry.

*Where was that blasted tea?*

Raven turned back to her text and ran her finger over the list of pressure points associated with asthmatic reactions, finding one that increased oxygen flow. She located the point on the chart. "Brit, please sit up as straight as you can and…" She cleared her throat. "And pull down the waistband of your trousers a bit."

Using every ounce of her training to stay removed from what she was doing, she placed her index finger on the taunt skin just below his belly button, found the spot, and placed the needle.

"I have the tea!" Mr. Thompson called as he bustled back into the room.

Raven let out a deep breath, as did her patient. Gathering her courage, she glanced at his face to see his color had returned with a vengeance, red staining his cheekbones. Raven bit her lip and jerked her eyes back to the diagram as Thompson handed Brit a cup of the stinging nettle tea. The strong earthy scent filled Raven's nose telling her he had brewed it correctly. "Thank you, Mr. Thompson."

She stood and assessed her patient with a critical eye. "Brit, please drink that tea as quickly as you may without burning your mouth."

He lifted the cup but arched a black brow in her direction.

After a moment, she realized he awaited her explanation of its purpose. "It will aid in opening your bronchial tubes and hasten the Laudanum through your system. You will need to drink the entire pot."

He gave a nod and began to drink the hot liquid.

Archie Fox materialized at her side and questioned with a note of pleading. "Is he going to make it?"

Raven watched Brit, his breath still wheezed, but his skin had begun to regain its true olive color. "Yes," she breathed in amazement. All the emotion she'd held back flooded her eyes. Before anyone could see, she turned and strode to the far side of the room and stopped in front of the window to gaze out at the wind-swept garden. The sun had begun to set, gilding the trees, and turning the few leaves still clinging to the maples a burnt orange.

She couldn't be sure if her patient had been someone else—someone with less physical strength and presence of mind—if she could've saved him. In truth of fact, she did not know how much of his recovery had been her doing or his own will. Either way, a prayer of thanksgiving flooded from her heart, and she knew she would never take the miracle of medicine for granted. Or the deep humility and gratitude that saving a life brought to her.

Her training as a nurse dictated that she have compassion but remain emotionally detached in order to make objective decisions. A dictate that she did not struggle with, customarily. But this man had had a strange effect on her. Perhaps the way he'd come after her when he'd first arrived had cracked her defenses. Or perhaps it was that he was special to everyone in the room—a rare individual who impacted lives in a way that didn't quickly fade. Brit...she realized she didn't even know his last name.

"Doc Cratchit, are *you* feeling all right?"

Composing herself, she turned around to face Chip. "Yes, I am well. And you?"

"I'm marvelous!"

Raven plucked a needle from just behind his ear as he asked, "Is Brit going to be all right?"

She nodded and glanced over at the man perched on the edge of a sofa that he made appear as if it belonged in a doll house. Needles poked out of his skin, but his breathing appeared steady as he spoke with the people gathered around him, including a group of young children and a large dog who'd entered the room when her back was turned. The newcomers began to speak over one another like a nest of magpies.

"Mr. Brit, are you okay?"

"What are those needles?"

"Where's yer clothes?"

"Do they hurt?"

"Are you sick?"

"Who put those stingers in you?"

The last question was stated in an angry demand that silenced the others. Brit appeared amused as he scratched his leg, and inhaled deeply, but Raven could not have her patient wasting his precious breath.

She stepped up to the circle of children. "Mr. Brit is going to be fine after more fluids and rest." She shifted her gaze to her patient. "Please continue to drink, sir."

Thompson snapped to attention and poured steaming tea into Brit's empty cup, and then shooed the children out of the room. The large dog, who at second glance, moved with the slowness of advanced age, stopped in front of Chip who tugged on his shirt and said, "Come on, Brom. Brit is in good hands." Chip followed after the younger children, reassuring his fellow classmates as he went. "That's Doc Cratchit. She helped me breathe again."

Raven found herself smiling.

"I must attend to the children." Mrs. March bowed her head to Raven. "I am immensely grateful to you, dear."

Raven dropped into a curtsy and Mrs. March shuffled away.

"Should we move him above stairs to his bed?" Mr. MacCarron called from the sofa.

"Yes, please do, Mr. MacCarron," Raven replied.

"After what's just transpired, call me Jack." His smile lit his blue gaze like the sky cleansed by a hard rain. "We don't stand on formalities here."

She smiled. "Jack, then."

"A wise physician, skill'd our wounds to heal, is more than armies to the public weal," her patient quoted before draining his cup.

"You've read Alexander Pope?" Raven couldn't hide her shock.

"Despite my earlier behavior, I'm not a Neanderthal, Miss Cratchit." Brit's mouth kicked up on one side and her heart did an odd little dance.

"He teaches English and Literature here at Hill House," Jack clarified. "Or at least, he did."

"Still do." Brit stood and began to pull needles from his skin. "I need to go."

"No, sir!" Raven blocked his path and crossed her arms, forced to look up to meet her patient's gaze. "Your condition is quite precarious."

"Go where?" Jack demanded.

"Back to Wexford House to confront my blasted brothers." Brit jerked the needle from his collarbone. "I'm quite grateful, Miss..."

His dark gaze met hers and she noticed purple rimmed his eyes, the skin around his strong, full lips appeared pale. "I am Miss Raven Cratchit. Did you say Wexford House?"

Brit swayed a bit and sunk back to the sofa. Raven sat beside him and poured him the last of the stinging nettle brew.

"Aye, I said Wexford House. Do you know it?"

Raven, for reasons she could not fathom, did not disclose her betrothal, but replied in a vague, "Well, yes, everyone in society knows Wexford House. What business do you have there? Are you acquainted with the Griffins?"

Brit's brows lowered and the ironic smirk that twisted his mouth transformed his attractive visage into an angry mask. "Haven't you heard? I'm the long-lost Earl of bloody Wexford."

# Chapter Four

*A lone caroler's sweet voice drifted to the boy through the crisp night air. "Silent night, holy night...All is calm. All is bright." The words of the ancient song lit a long-ago recollection of happiness and family, the details just beyond the boy's grasp. A contrast to his current circumstances so sharp that he pushed his feet faster lest the tears freeze upon his cheeks. It was Christmas Eve.*

*The bell tolled four...*

Brit watched wonder play across Raven Cratchit's face. He drank in her dark-fringed eyes and the glossy black sweep of her hair, and noted a warmth in the set of her full-lipped mouth and a vast intelligence behind her gaze that radiated a vivacity beyond mere beauty.

"*You* are the missing earl?" she questioned with more than a touch of shock.

"Pray, attempt to hide your amazement. You wound me," he quipped as he placed a fist over his heart. But his sarcasm cost him, and his breath shuddered in his chest.

"That's it!" Jack thundered. "I'm escorting you to your bed."

Raven peered into Brit's eyes as if she could see his very brain. Brit realized he thought of her as Raven, not Miss Cratchit or Doc Cratchit as Chip favored. He could blame his lack of decorum on his illness but suspected it had more to do with the woman herself.

"Yes, do," she urged. Then after a brief hesitation, inquired, "Pardon me for asking, but how do you know? You are actually he...the lost earl?"

"Jack did a bit of sleuthing and found that my parents were Lord and Lady Wexford. A solicitor confirmed his findings and presented me with all the necessary papers. It is true." Even if Brit didn't wish it.

"Brit, that's incredible!" Raven exclaimed, her face, her lips, her velvet-draped knee far closer than propriety dictated.

A slow smile spread across his mouth at her use of his Christian name. Perhaps the life-saving bond extended in both directions; a connection which superseded the hideous constraints society would place upon them.

As if she read his thoughts, her eyes darted to his still bare chest then down to their joined knees, and she lurched back. "Pardon me, Lord Wexford."

Something dark simmered inside him at the sound of the title, but he fought it back as he measured his next words. "Did you know the Griffins had a half brother who had gone missing?"

"Yes. Actually, the missing Earl of Wexford is a legend among high society."

Brit lifted a brow. "Do tell."

Raven opened a wooden box fitted with multiple trays and containing tiny slots for each of the individual needles she'd used. She balanced the kit upon her lap and turned to him, her gaze clinical as she plucked the hair-thin apparatus sticking out of his wrist. "Stories of the missing earl have circulated for years, each more outrageous than the last. One popular theory was that the young earl..." She glanced up at his face and corrected herself. "That *you* became lost in the forest and were eaten by wolves."

After removing another needle from his arm and placing it in the corresponding slot, she continued. "Some say you were a changeling and spirited away by fairies. While others insist you were born with such a horrible deformity that your parents locked you in a secret room at their country seat and then claimed you had gone missing."

Brit and Jack exchanged a telling glance over Raven's head. The two of them had developed a relationship that often did not require words. And Brit easily read his own affront reflected in his mentor's darkening gaze. As a young Brit had starved in the streets, thieving to survive one more day, the gentry of London had toasted their well-turned-out toes by warm hearths whilst sipping tea and fabricating fantastical fictions about his life. He did not consider himself a sensitive sort of fellow, but it was almost too much to reconcile.

"Are you acquainted with my...er..." Brit almost choked on the word. "...brothers, John and George, then?"

"Yes," she replied without raising her gaze.

"What did they claim had become of me?"

Raven removed the last needle from his skin and lifted her gaze. "John?"

Brit gave a tight nod, unwilling to examine the sudden churn of his gut at her familiar address or the reddening of her cheeks.

"He has always made his position clear that it would not be discussed. He considered the topic…unseemly." Her chin took on a firm set. "I do not believe for a moment that he would harm you if that is what you are thinking. I have been under the impression that he and George were quite devastated by the loss of their brother…the loss of you."

Brit searched her face. He had not expressed his belief that John had attempted to poison his tea. In the limited experience he'd had with ladies of high society—as she obviously was—they did not think far past the end of their well-powdered noses. But she had ascertained his suspicion and refuted it in such a way that he was tempted to believe her.

She closed her kit, stood, and in a formal tone, said, "My professional recommendation is that you rest for the next two days, Lord Wexford. Which means do not get out of bed except to use the water closet. Your body has sustained a serious trauma and needs to recover."

"I cannot stay in bed for…" But even as Brit protested, a wave of fatigue washed over him, forcing his eyes closed as the room spun.

"I'll fetch Thompson," Jack said, striding out of the room. "I'm going to need assistance dragging your sorry arse up two flights of stairs."

The unchaperoned moment stretched into silence until Raven hefted a large tome, and said, "Make sure to drink as much as you can over the next day to flush the Laudanum from your system."

Brit nodded as he cracked an eye open and took in her formal velvet gown. "Have I kept you from a social engagement?"

"Well, I—"

"You look a bit dragged out, mate."

Brit would recognize Archie's sarcasm anywhere. "Better than you on a good day, Fox."

"The illness has deluded him, poor beggar." Archie shook his head at Raven.

"Indeed," she agreed with an impish smile.

"Ugh…take me to my bed then. I might as well give up on life," Brit sighed.

Raven's unguarded laughter spilled out like silvery bells, reviving Brit's strength. He stood, but Jack rushed into the room with Thompson, and they were instantly on either side to prop him up beneath his arms.

Fox was nowhere to be found.

Brit shook his head. Had Archie been in the room, or had he imagined the entire conversation? In his current state, he couldn't be certain. Vision spinning, he turned to Jack. "I'll take a short rest. But that's all I can promise."

"I would think the opportunity to have us wait upon you hand and foot would appeal to you, kid," Jack commented.

Jack was only ten years Brit's senior and at least a head shorter than him, so the nickname was more predilection than classification.

When Raven gave a disbelieving chuckle, Jack turned a smile her way. "Brit and I go way back. Don't we, mate?"

"That we do, old man," Brit patted him on the chest. "That we do."

Raven had donned a long black coat with a fur collar that tickled the line of her delicate jaw. "I feel you are in capable hands, Lord Wexford. Please send word if you or Chip require further treatment."

As Jack thanked her, Brit's voice froze in his throat. But it wasn't his shortness of breath that stopped him from speaking. He simply did not have the words. The unique woman's vivid gaze locked on his for a count of three before she turned on the heel of her sensible boot and walked out.

Raven stopped on the covered stoop and watched the first snow of the season drift down in lazy flakes. Whilst she had worked, the world had transformed; the dingy fog crystallized into a flurry of stars. The lawn, hedgerow, and boughs of feathery firs sparkled in shimmering dust. She pushed out a sigh and exhaled her tension one frosty breath at a time. Two lives had been saved that day, but the rush had taken its toll. She felt exposed, vulnerable, and a bit shaky.

Her heart thrummed in her chest cavity, as it always had, but the beat had somehow changed. Like the throb of a song with a fresh tempo dancing through her veins. She couldn't say if it was from the emotional rush of her success, an over-production of her adrenal glands, or something more...something new.

She'd called for the phaeton to be brought 'round, but as she stepped onto the sugared walk, her feet crunching into perfect prints in the silvery glacé, she took another step. And then another. And another. She kept going until she'd passed the circle drive, crossed the front garden, and exited the gate to the street. Her fur-lined hood rested on her shoulders as snow melted against her heated cheeks, coating her hair and lashes.

Raven's parents and siblings awaited her at Wexford house where they would smile and laugh while toasting her 'joyous union,' as her mother liked to say. But in that moment, she could not portray the happy bride-to-be. She needed time to process. To re-center herself.

The lane wound down a gradual hill dotted with sprawling estates. The district was not fashionable, each manse in varying levels of disrepair. But the soft air, encapsulated by the snowfall, turned the ordinary street into a winter wonderland. Blessedly alone, a state she rarely found herself in and never out of doors, was bliss. No watching eyes, listening ears, questioning mouths. She could think and not arrange her face into a socially acceptable mien.

At the moment, her expression likely reflected her shock and awe. She had just met the lost Earl of *bloody* Wexford, as he had so articulately described himself. Laughter escaped her chest, the sound echoing back to her in icy fumes. With no one around to judge her, she tilted her head back and opened her mouth, catching crisp, cold flakes on her tongue. Something like wings flapped and heated her belly.

*Lord Brit Griffin.*

Every time Raven thought his name, his handsome visage appeared before her mind's eye and her cheeks caught fire. The man had thundered into her life with the elegance of a rampaging elephant, trampling her precepts of science and shattering defenses she hadn't realized she'd erected around herself. Her heartbeat tripped forward again. She took deep, slow breaths to regulate her pulse. As a woman of learning, not useless sentiment, she could not account for her frenzied state. But out there all alone in the frozen countryside, she indulged in a moment of undisciplined, deliciously emotional analysis.

He was unlike anyone she'd yet encountered. His gentlemanly façade—and quite a fine façade it was—battled with something untamed and far from predictable. Most men of her age were complete dullards, perfect gentlemen with irrefutable manners and tedious dispositions. She and Belinda had invented a secret game where they would amuse themselves at parties, by predicting the next words spoken by a given gentleman. Ninety percent of the time, they were correct, if off by a word choice or two.

*"I declare, you have the...bluest eyes I've seen in an age...the creamiest skin...the shiniest hair."*

*"My horse is the best stock...my curricle is the fastest...my country estate...my...my...my..."*

Not that all men were dimwits, but for what reason Raven could not surmise, the men of her class seemed to mimic one another in effect, speech, and even dress like a parade of well-turned-out penguins. Perhaps that was why John Griffin had caught her attention. He had a jovial disposition and did not prevaricate regarding his opinions.

But Brit Griffin was something else entirely. A paradox of sharp intelligence, fierce determination, wicked wit, and something a bit...wild. As if the parlor was not his natural habitat, in fact, could barely contain him. He'd assured her he was no Neanderthal, and yet, as he'd lay close to death, she'd glimpsed a primeval constitution. The ferocity of a warrior.

Lost in thought, her slipper hit a patch of ice and she pitched back, landing hard on the sidewalk. Heart in her throat, she sat dumbly for a moment as her bottom throbbed. Perhaps silk slippers were not the thing for a winter walk. Belinda would absolutely gaff if she saw her little sister sprawled in the snowfall, noble blue skirts spattered with slush. With a soft smile, Raven assessed herself for injuries, and determining herself fit, steadied her hands on the icy ground.

But before she could gather her legs beneath her, a soft tinkle like a bell rang through the frosty air and a gloved hand appeared, fingers extended for assistance. She started and her gaze snapped up to find an older gentleman bent over her, eyes the silvery gray of sleet. Where had he come from? Raven had been quite certain she was alone.

Years of tutelage in proper societal decorum made her raise her hand to accept the stranger's assistance. The old man smiled as he tugged her to her feet with surprising strength. He did not appear well turned out, stringy gray hair poking from beneath a dilapidated top hat and ruddy cheeks stained with cold or dirt—or perhaps both—framed a pointed nose and wiry chin. But despite his obvious lack of status, the man glowed with good intentions and a warmth of the familiar, although she felt certain they had never met.

Raven returned his smile as he released her hand. "Thank you, kind sir."

"Of course, Miss." He tipped his hat to reveal a frosty rime about his balding head, and holes in tattered gloves.

The chill of the air apparent in shivers that chased down her back, Raven's concern sharpened. "Good sir, may I offer you some assistance?"

If the Cratchits were known for anything, it was their generosity. Her father enjoyed going to market, especially this time of year, and finding a family without means so that he could buy them a carton brimming with food and whatever gifts he could heap upon them. Just last week, Mrs. Cratchit had invited a woman off the street to sleep in the house and ended up finding her a suitable position in a neighboring household. Peter treated those who could not pay him for a cup of watered brandy or a hand-knitted scarf, which he would turn around and gift to a child on the street. Charity resided in the Cratchit's very blood. "We have a warm spare room in our home that you are welcome to," she continued in earnest.

"Very kind, very kind," the vagrant muttered as he cocked a fuzzy brow and gave a decisive nod. "As I suspected."

"Suspected?" For the first time, Raven realized it was after dark and she'd forgotten her muff. The skin of her hands ached with cold through the damp kid leather of her gloves, and she could barely feel her toes.

Gaze twinkling, the elderly man asked, "You just left Hill House, did you not?"

"Yes, actually," she replied. "Treating a patient there. Well, two."

"Young Chip and strapping Brit, I presume?"

"Why yes, are you acquainted?"

"Quite." The word came out as a chuckle.

Unsure of the joke, Raven steered the conversation back to the man's predicament. "My family can offer you shelter for the night. Or will you at least accept a hearty meal?"

He cocked his head, visage alight, as if inspecting a bit of treasure he'd found nestled in a forgotten corner. "Intelligent. Spirited. Kind." He gazed up into the clear sky, stars winking back at him. "I believe she'll do nicely."

A bit unsettled by the man's random prattle, Raven glanced behind her and up the road. Candles flickered in the windows of a nearby manor house that appeared neglected but habitable. Perhaps the man didn't require her assistance after all. She turned back. "Is that your home—" Her words cut off abruptly.

The old vagabond had vanished.

Without a trace. Not even a footfall in the freshly fallen snow marked his passage.

Raven spun in a tight circle, taking in the desolate scenery. A chill that had little to do with the cold traced down her spine. "Sir?" Her voice echoed as flurries fell, stinging her cheeks.

With a shake of her head, she turned around and began to walk the way she'd come. Her father had taught her long ago that she could not help those who did not wish for assistance. Although harmless, that man clearly suffered from dementia of the brain and likely did not wish to end up in Bedlam. Not that she could blame him. The barbaric practices of the mental hospital were well known. Raven walked on and said a quick prayer that the man had shelter and someone to care for him.

Cold, tired, and a little lost, she trudged on in search of signs of Hill Orphanage. Had she turned at the cross street or walked straight? And where had her head gone anyway? Silly girlish fantasies, that's where! Brit Griffin may be mythical in his return from the dead, but he was just a man. Plain and simple.

Before she could decide which direction to take, the smart tap of hooves echoed through the evening air, preceding the phaeton as it came into view around the bend. Gus stood in his seat and pulled the horse to a stop. "Miss Cratchit, whot you doin' there?"

A cloud crystalized as she breathed a sigh of relief. "Sorry, Mr. Gus. I needed a bit of fresh air."

His face folded in gruff lines of disapproval before he smoothed his expression and asked, "Where to, Miss?"

Raven didn't think long, crashing from her emotional rush, energy leeched from her limbs until she felt like a doll made of rags. "Home, please." Her warmest dressing gown, a nice cup of peppermint tea, and a light book of mysteries were just the medicine she needed.

The old driver folded out the stairs and took her hand to assist her onto the seat. "Lose a patient, did ye?"

Raven stared at the man's weathered face in surprise, then remembered he'd driven Peter to house calls for years before she'd started her medical practice. He flipped out his coat and settled beside her, turning to her with expectancy.

"The opposite actually. I saved a boy and a man. Both from varying degrees of respiratory distress. But..."

Before she could gather her thoughts as to how to explain, Gus said, "Get a bit of a 'igh from it, dontcha? 'at's whot Doc Peter always says."

"Precisely," Raven answered as she tucked the waiting lap blanket around her legs and Gus snapped the reins, jerking the cart into motion. Conducting a personal conversation of any sort with a servant was decidedly improper, something most in the gentry would never consider. Then again, the Cratchits defied most norms in high society.

For much of her childhood, they had been as poor as church mice in an underprivileged parish. Most evenings were spent huddled around the one fire they could afford to fuel, where they would share a meal rationed among them; a small roast chicken lasting the family of eight two to three days. Tiny Tim would often suck on the bones after the skin and meat had been consumed. But Mother and Father never let them feel deprived. Father was fond of saying, "As long as we have God and each other, we have love. That's more than some of the wealthiest families possess."

Her mother had taken in laundry to earn extra money, and the family would make a singing game out of helping her wash and scrub. When Father arrived home before nightfall, they would play Charades or Squeak Piggy Squeak or tournaments of chess with a set he'd inherited from his grandfather.

Even through Tim's illness, her parents maintained their gratitude. If she overheard her mother crying sometimes at night, the next morning she would be all smiles. And if Tim got a few more hugs or an extra sweet, none of them begrudged him.

Then, one miraculous Christmas morning, Ebenezer Scrooge turned their lives around. After bringing them more food than they usually ate in a fortnight, and toys—oh, the glorious toys—he made Father his partner. Their business not only multiplied exponentially, but because of all the service they did for the poor of the city, Queen Victoria knighted both her father and Mr. Scrooge before he passed. Raven barely remembered their old benefactor, but he lived on as a saint in tales told around the fire.

Now their family was accepted in high society along with old wealth and the aristocracy of London's elite who normally snubbed rich merchants as upstarts. That, along with her father's honorary title, had allowed her to make such a smart match with the Earl of Wexford.

Who, she realized with a start, was no longer an earl at all now that his brother had returned from the dead. Had John told her family at dinner? She knew her father didn't give a fig about titles, he only wanted her well-treated and happy. But still. It must have been quite a surprise to them all. Each of their faces flashed before her as she predicted their reactions around the dinner table; her oldest sister, Martha would soak up every juicy detail to relay to her friends (which Raven would need to put a stop to posthaste), Peter would remain stoic, Matthew would be empathetic, Tim amused, her mother shocked, and her father...her father would wish to know how *she* felt about it. But each one of them would rally around her with whatever support she needed. Including Belinda, in her way, who would question Raven until she broke down and confessed all.

Above and through all things, The Cratchits stuck together. Which made them quite an extraordinary family.

As they turned a corner, a squall blew flakes that had turned glacial into her face, the cold seeping into her bones. Abandoning her dreams of a roaring fire and a book nestled in her lap, Raven shouted over the wind, "Gus, I've changed my mind. Take me to Wexford House in Mayfair."

# Chapter Five

*A family, so large they blocked the walk, forced the boy into the muck-filled street. He counted six children of various ages, the youngest a frail boy carried in his father's arms. Their clothes were ragged, not much better than his own, but they laughed and talked excitedly, one of the girls lifting her voice in song. As the boy rounded the group, he met the singing girl's periwinkle gaze. Of their own accord his feet slowed, and he tipped his cap to her. She smiled. And for a moment, the world fell silent.*

*The bell tolled five...*

Brit woke with a start, drenched in sweat, heart racing as if he were sprinting to beat that cursed church bell once again. *Blimey.* He hadn't thought about that wretched night in ages. Old Scrooge and his blasted stew. For so many reasons, none of them good, that man had changed the course of his life.

Brit ran a hand over his face and opened burning eyes. The parted draperies admitted a golden beam of sun that traversed the dark wood floor, cut across the blue and brown wool rug, and

up his crammed floor-to-ceiling bookcase, lighting the spines of
*Gulliver's Travels, The Corsair, Robinson Crusoe,* and *The Legend
of Sleepy Hollow.* The beloved titles grounded him in the present.
Each tome chosen with care to add to his ever-expanding collection. It was his only extravagance beyond a new suit each year and
shoes every season.

The MacCarrons paid him a generous salary that he budgeted
to the penny. He set aside ten percent for personal expenses, such
as clothing or the occasional foray into the City, ten percent for
books, and eighty percent went directly into his savings account.
As long as he lived at the orphanage, his room and board cost
him nothing, and he'd learned long ago to have a contingency
plan for all possible outcomes. His nest egg gave him comfort and
shut down the street kid that yammered inside him whenever he
purchased a gift or rare book.

Brit shivered and noticed the fire had faded to embers. A glance
at the clock on his bedside table told him he'd slept through the
night and into late morning. Shocked by his self-indulgence, he
threw back the covers and sat up, only to have a sharp pain grip
his brain. That was when the memory of his near death, and subsequent treatment by the captivating Raven Cratchit, forced him
back to his pillow.

The woman's enchanting face and the memory of her soothing
touch gave way to the knowledge that he was *still* the Earl of bloody
Wexford, and his newly found brothers had attempted to murder
him. A rancid start to his day to be sure.

He squeezed his eyes closed again. "She should have let me die."

"No way I'm letting that happen, mate."

Brit squinted enough to watch Chip carry a tray of food into the room, the boy's blond curls clean and shiny, his skin glowing with health. Brit let out a sigh of relief and then a realization made him demand, "Why are you not restricted to bedrest?"

Chip set the tray on the table and propped his hands on his hips, freckled nose in the air. "Because I have the constitution of a bull."

Bracing himself for the pain this time, Brit rose to prop himself up on an elbow. "And what does that make me?"

"A foul pig based on the stench you're puttin' off!" The boy moved to the window, threw open the drapes, and lifted the window to let in a blast of frigid air.

"I'll admit a bath may be in order." Gingerly, Brit sat up and planted his feet on the floor. Like a newborn colt, he stood, made his slow, dizzy way to the sitting area, and flopped into his cushioned reading chair. "If you insist upon opening the blasted window, at least stoke up the fire."

"Aye, your mighty Lordship," Chip quipped with a bow.

"Ugh...not you too." Brit slid lower in his seat. "I thought at least you would not alter your opinion of me. I'm no more a Lord than you are."

After throwing a few planks of wood into the grate and stoking up the flames, Chip turned around, his face an odd combination of concern and resolve. "But you are an earl, ain't you?"

Brit took the opportunity to down a glass of juice, the cool liquid soothing his head instantly. The boy sat in the chair opposite him and stared him down unblinking. An intimidation tactic Brit had taught him a bit too well.

The night he'd met Chip had been one of the worst storms Brit had ever experienced. Streets in the slums flooded quickly, creating rivers of garbage and human waste. He'd scored a fat wallet at the first strike of lightning and then three more as the lily-livered toffs struggled with brollies and scurried for higher ground. His coat bulging with loot, he'd skipped through the rain, whistling a tune in anticipation of sharing his windfall with Archie and the rest of the gang, when he'd heard a baby's cry. He'd stopped in the middle of the street, icy water sloshing into his boots, and seen a toddler crouched in the doorway of Barnard's Inn.

A lump of a man stuck his head out the door. "I told ye, I ain't got nothin' for a street rat. Now move on!" He'd slammed the door with such force the wood hit the child's back, knocking the sobs right out of him.

As Brit had drawn closer, he could see the boy was no more than four or five years old, the rags that hung on his spindly arms caked in filth. "Are you hungry?" he had asked without preamble.

Blue eyes the size of saucers had lifted at Brit's voice and the tiny boy gave a nod, his chest heaving.

"Come on, then." At Brit's gesture, Chip had followed him all the way to his hideout without another peep.

They'd been thick as thieves ever since. Quite literally. Brit had taught Chip everything he'd known about the craft of thieving, and the boy had taken to it like a Copper to the pastry shop. Reversing the process had proved a bit more difficult. No matter how many etiquette lessons Mrs. March put Chip through, he still clung to many habits from his past; the reticence to trust, the charm that disarmed and manipulated.

"First off, if Mrs. M heard you say 'ain't' she would tan your hide." Brit picked up a crispy piece of bacon and took a bite. "Secondly, yes, I am the heir to an earldom."

Chip leaned forward eagerly. "How rich are you?"

Brit thought of the properties and assets Mr. Veck had listed, and his head spun. He closed his eyes for a moment, unsure if the dizziness was rooted in his ailment or the shock he still experienced at his shift in identity. He'd never seen himself as more than a street kid who lucked into a cushy position with the MacCarrons. Unlike Chip, he'd taken to decorum lessons with unnatural ease. Or quite naturally, as it turned out, given his parentage. He'd thrived in the academic environment as well; partial to stories that expanded his mind to other times, worlds, and people he would never have occasion to meet, stories of relationships layered and complex, mysteries both thrilling and hopeful. Now he had the privilege of introducing his students to the books that had shaped his life, and he taught them how to use words to fashion their own destinies far from the destitution of London's ghettos.

Even if Olivia believed he was squandering his potential, as she'd often said when she'd encouraged him to find a position outside of the orphanage, he would miss watching the children's faces light up when they read their first words or when they heard a story that expanded their limited perspective. Henceforth, his life would consist of managing properties, handling assets, and fulfilling his noble obligation to sit in The House of Lords. Dry, logical, practical duty.

"Should I send for the Doc?" Chip asked.

Brit's eyes popped open. "No. I'm quite all right." To prove it, he picked up his plate and shoved a forkful of eggs into his mouth. The last thing he needed was a blasted crow poking and prodding him. Even if that crow bore more resemblance to a graceful starling. He gulped down a mouthful of weak tea, disgusted by his sappy thoughts.

"I'm feeling better by the moment. And to answer your earlier question, yes, I am now richer than King Midas...if..." He set down his plate with a plunk. "I marry by Christmas."

"*This* Christmas?"

Brit nodded.

"In four weeks?" Chip leaned forward and set his elbows on his knees.

"Yes."

"What happens if you don't?"

"My fortune and the earldom revert to my nearest male relation. Which, it would seem, is my half brother John." Brit ran a hand over his face, part of him wondering if he cared all that much. The money and power did not move him, but his parent's legacy, the only thing that connected him to his birth family...*that* he could get behind. He would fulfill his birthright if only to honor them.

"Millie down at the bakery always gives you an extra sweet bun," Chip said as he attempted to pinch a piece of bacon from Brit's plate. Brit smacked his knuckles, the meat falling neatly back to the salver.

Chip sat back, undeterred. "Helga, the governess next door stops by at least once a week to *borrow* a book from you. And the butcher's daughter hangs around after her deliveries until she speaks to you personal-like."

Amused by the boy's matchmaking efforts, Brit chuckled. "Chip, I cannot marry just anyone..."

"What about Miss Olivia's cousin, Violet's younger sister? She's..." He moved his hands in the shape of an hourglass and wiggled his brows.

"It has nothing to do with appearance, Chip. I now have to marry a highborn lady."

"Why?" The boy grimaced comically.

"My future wife will become a..." He thought for a moment on the proper title. "Countess."

Chip's face crumpled. "You're truly leaving us, then?"

Brit stared at this boy who was more a brother to him than the Griffins ever could be, and his heart gave a lurch. "Yes, as soon as I am able. But I promise I'll come back at least twice a week. And you can come visit me." The thought of the rough and tumble orphan cruising around the Griffins' upscale Mayfair townhome, wreaking havoc with the servants and his half brothers, lifted Brit's spirits considerably. "Yes. First opportunity, I will have you come for an extended stay."

"I could never fit into some noble toff's household." Chip stared at the floor dejectedly.

"Nor will I, but it'll be a right sight us trying, won't it?" Brit grinned wickedly and waved the last bit of bacon under Chip's nose. Who, never one to turn down an offer of food of any sort, snatched it and shoved it into his mouth.

"That it will, my good man." A mischievous smile that Brit knew well lit up Chip's eyes. "That it will!"

"Well, that was a certified nightmare," Belinda said by way of greeting as she barged into Raven's room without so much as a good afternoon. "Not that you care," she continued, flouncing into a chair by the hearth.

Raven finished writing the sentence in her journal where she documented her medical successes and failures and then placed the pen back in its stand before turning in her desk chair. "By the time I arrived, everyone had already gone."

"Did you at least speak to Lord Wexford? Explain why you could not be bothered to show up to your own engagement dinner?"

Raven opened her mouth to correct Belinda on John Griffin's title change and then closed it again. Had he not told her family about his lost brother's return? And why not? Surely if he had shared such a juicy tidbit of gossip, Bel would've woken her at dawn and badgered her for details.

"Why do you appear as if you've swallowed a slug?" Belinda asked tartly.

When Raven did not answer, her sister continued. "It was dreadfully awkward, you know. Sitting around the dinner table, Mother and Father trying to speak around the elephant missing from the room." She smirked. "So to speak."

"Yes, I imagine it was," Raven replied as her mind turned back to a pair of midnight-dark eyes fastened to her face as he fought for life, an invisible cord knitting between them with each hard-won breath. Stories spun behind that gaze, so much life lived in Brit's short years. What circumstances had carved the hardship and pain around his mouth? The strength and hope in his gaze? How had he ended up teaching literature at Hill Orphanage? Where had he been all of these missing years? And more importantly, why hadn't she told him she was betrothed to his brother?

The missing Earl of Wexford, indeed.

"Lucy Anne Cratchit, please attend the conversation at hand!"

Raven's gaze whipped to her sister's face who had just channeled their mother with such clarity that Raven's stomach dropped as it did when she'd broken the rules and discipline was about to befall her. In which case, their parents always addressed her by her name given at birth. *Lucy Anne* spoke of preciousness and frills, which did not suit her in the least. Thus, the nickname her late grandmother had coined in reference to her hair being 'as black as a raven's wing' had stuck.

"That's better. Now, please tell me what has you so abstracted," Bel prompted.

Raven turned fully around. "Did John not tell the family any-thing...interesting last night?"

Belinda's mouth twisted in perplexity. "Interesting? Other than the new land he acquired in Brighton? Or the horseflesh he trav-eled to Shropshire to preview? Or some political pish-posh about The International Workingmen's Association he and Father de-bated all through the entrée course." Her gray eyes brightened. "Oh sister, you should have seen the ham croquettes!"

Raven smiled. They both shared a healthy—or perhaps more precisely, an obsessive—love of food. No doubt due to the lack thereof in their early childhood. The Griffins' new French chef, who it was rumored John had paid an exorbitant salary to leave *un restaurant très chic* in Paris, had the gentry in a whirl. Distract-ed by their shared passion, Raven questioned, "And the pudding course?"

"Absolutely divine! A stunning crystal trifle with layers of sherry-soaked cake, jam, custard, and whipped cream, topped with fresh berries from the Griffin's hot house." She wilted into her chair with a long-enduring sigh.

"I am truly sorry about not being there. When I arrived, you had all left and John had gone to his gentleman's club."

Not one to sit still for long, Belinda began to wander about the room, stopping at Raven's dressing table and lifting her ring-stand. "Are you ever going to wear his ring?" She picked up the gold ensemble of three large gems; an enormous round emerald flanked by two square-cut sapphires.

Raven turned back to her medical notebook, grasped her pen, dipped it in ink, and began writing. "It is too large for practicality."

"He wears your ring. And your hair in a locket on his watch-chain."

"How do you know?" Raven asked without looking up. She'd just remembered to note the exact ratio of the nettle tea preparation she'd given Brit.

"I saw it hanging beside his watch the twenty times he pulled it from his pocket to check the time during dinner. Do you at least wear the necklace he gave you?"

"It itches my skin. I never could abide silver."

"Does your locket match his?"

"Er...yes?"

"I knew it! You didn't purchase his engagement ring or the locket. Mother did! Did she sneak in here and clip a lock of your hair while you slept?"

Raven spun around. "I don't know what you expect from me. I'm not prone to flights of fancy. Like some I know." Her cheeks heated as she remembered her earlier thoughts about the new Earl of Wexford.

"That is low, sister. Perhaps if you had taken your nose out of your books long enough to know love, you would not condemn me for my depth of feeling!" Belinda crossed her arms under her chest and turned her face away, but not before Raven noticed a shimmer of tears.

"I'm sorry, Bel. Truly." She stood and implored her sister. "Look at me, please."

She turned, her bottom lip trembling.

"You are vivacious and spirited. There's nothing wrong with that and I did not mean to imply differently. I know you're still hurting. That ass, Lord Eaton likely already regrets losing the best thing that ever happened to him. Married to that dried-up old baroness."

"Raven!" Bel squawked. "That is unkind in the extreme." But her mouth twitched, and her eyes regained their twinkle.

Compelled to make up for all her shortcomings, Raven motioned Belinda over to the bed. "I have a secret."

Bel's eyes lit up like Christmas candles as she threw herself upon the coverlet, propping her head in her hand. "Ohhh...do tell!"

"Only if you promise upon pain of death that you will not tell a soul." Raven knew she would not tell anyone, but still claimed the vow they used to make to one another as children.

"There are other things more painful," Bel muttered, but then sat up and gave a solemn nod. "I have nothing of value to offer."

A token had always been given to the person telling the secret and if the other divulged their confidence, they had the right to either keep or destroy the other's prized possession. Raven met her sister's gaze. "This is a secret worth far more than a hair ribbon or even a book. But the truth will likely leak out soon enough, so I will accept your word as your vow."

"Yes, I promise. Now get on with it!" Bel bounced up and down on the mattress.

"Yesterday after I treated the child at Hill Orphanage, another man stumbled through the doors on the brink of death. He was out of his mind and attempted to attack me. He was so large and powerfully built that it took two men to hold him back."

Bel's hands flew to her cheeks. "Why would he do such a thing?"

"Well, I soon discovered he'd had an adverse reaction to Laudanum that was impairing his breathing...and his judgment."

"Oh, my!"

"Once he had been calmed, he would not allow me to bleed him because as a child he had watched as his mother died while being bled. I was forced to use unconventional treatments, a combination of herbs, acupuncture, and breathing techniques that..."

Belinda waved her hand in a circular motion, not the least interested in a medical lecture.

"Yes, well, it turns out the man is a teacher of literature at the orphanage and just discovered his true identity as..." She took a deep breath and her sister leaned forward. "He is the lost Earl of Wexford."

Bel reared back, her eyes wide. "No!"

"Yes, I believe it is true."

"The mad earl who was locked away until he took his own life?"

"That is a rumor, Bel."

"John and George Griffin's lost half brother?"

"Yes."

"Then that means...this man is the true Earl. Not John," Bel asserted.

"Perhaps."

"Where has he been? What happened to him?"

"I am not certain." Raven shook her head and then thought, *But I'd really like to know.*

Belinda clutched her hands in front of her chest, her eyes going starry. "What's he like?"

To her intense mortification, Raven felt heat rush up her neck and into her face. "He is..." How could she describe his presence? His fierce strength? His unconventional appeal? Her words and feelings clashed and crumbled inside her head until she said, "He is...different."

"Well, that's articulate." Her sister rolled her eyes, then really looked at her. "Wait. Why are you blushing?"

Raven's next words popped out before she could stop them. "I saw his naked chest."

"Oh! Now we're getting somewhere!" Belinda rubbed her hands together in anticipation.

"It's not like that." Raven rose from the bed and opened her wardrobe to search for her boots. Or perhaps to hide the deepening of her blush. Brit's chest, smooth skin over hard muscle, had not strayed far from her thoughts in the last twenty-four hours. She'd seen more than her share of unclothed men. She had two brothers after all, but they were thin and pale. And, well...her brothers. She'd treated many males working alongside Peter, none of which had caused the stirring of her attention. "He had to partially disrobe for me to treat him. It was purely in the name of science."

"Purely." Bel drew out the word, so it sounded like the purr of a cat. Then her eyes widened. "What does Lord Griffin think of his brother's return?"

Raven sunk into her desk chair, smacked down by a mortifying realization. Not once, since meeting Brit Griffin, had she thought about John's feelings. She'd rushed to her engagement dinner with thoughts for her family. And for herself, to save face, if truth be told. But with the appearance of the rightful heir, John very well may lose his title, his fortune, his very identity.

"Peter is attending at Newgate, so my afternoon is free," Raven said contemplatively. "But I need moral support when I go to Wexford House." She paused in pulling on her boot and lowered her brows in a stern expression. "One who will *not* wag her tongue regarding the missing earl's return."

"Reporting for duty." Bel snapped her heels together and lifted her hand to her head in salute. "No one listens to me anyway. But I'll only accompany you if we can go Christmas shopping after. New Bond Street is glorious this time of year!"

"Of course," Raven answered with a chuckle even as her stomach knotted in dread. How much more of her absenteeism would John take? And how did he feel about his long-lost brother coming back from the dead to claim his title? Whether she felt ready or not, she would find out soon.

# Chapter Six

*The boy raced down the street, less than a block from Scrooge House. So close, yet so far. His short legs pumped like steam engine pistons, but he wasn't fast enough. He had begun to despair when he spied a carriage hitched to twin steeds stamping clouds of snow. A whip cracked above their heads and as they trotted off, the boy shifted the stew to his left arm, swerved behind the vehicle, and latched onto the bar of the mudguard. Wheels churned slush, splashing arcs as they found traction, dragging the boy behind. His boots slid along the icy road. Faster and faster.*

*The bell tolled six...*

Later that afternoon when Raven arrived at Wexford House, she found the household in a flurry of holiday preparations and John not at home. Sadness hitched in her chest to see the harried servants rushing to deck the halls, doing their duty like soldiers on a mission. Where was the joy of the season? Gingerbread baking in the oven. Competitions for the most well-turned-out tree? The laughter? For the Cratchit family, Christmas trimming was practically a national holiday.

"You may wait in the parlor if you like, Miss Cratchit," Grant, the Griffins' butler kindly offered as he tucked her card into his pocket.

Raven shifted to find her sister's eyes at half mast, chin tilted just so, her lips pursed, one corner curled in a kittenish grin. Belinda liked to model her flirtation skills for Raven, hoping they might wear off someday. Bel complained that science had permeated Raven's brain causing her to appear more automaton than young woman.

Trying to observe her sister as an outsider, Raven noted that Bel's nose was a bit too pronounced for most to consider pretty, her mouth a fraction too wide, and her figure a bit too shapely for convention. But her warmth and vivacity, her insatiable zest for life, had always drawn the eye of every man she had encountered.

In experimentation, Raven mimicked her sister's coquettish expression and popped out a hip, placing a hand on the smallest part of her waist. Grant did a double-take, his pale-blue eyes taking on a dazed quality as one end of the ribbon-strewn garland he held tumbled to the floor.

Face heating in shame, Raven wiped her expression clean and straightened. "Thank you, Grant. If you expect Lor—" Her throat closed on the title John no longer held, only a sharp elbow from Belinda restarting her speech. "...Lord Wexford home within the hour, then I shall wait."

The man gave a nod, his balding head catching a shine from the hanging candelabra as he turned on his heel. "Follow me, if you please."

Once ensconced in the parlor, promised refreshments on the way, Raven lowered to a delicate chintz sofa patterned with large flowers, the ornate legs painted gold. "Honestly, Bel, your flirtation is akin to a weapon."

Belinda sat across from her and tapped a finger to her lips. "I would liken it more to an art. One that takes practice to perfect. Your attempt on the butler was clumsy at best."

"Well, I certainly have no need of such arts when I already have a fiancé," Raven said primly.

"Ah..." Bel leaned back and arched a single brow. "But how do you plan to keep him? Even husbands long for a bit of mystery."

"Perhaps," Raven said, dismissing the topic as she observed the recently remodeled room. Watered silk paper covered the walls in a veritable forest complete with exotic creatures and towering reeds of bamboo. Touches of the East were everywhere. A carved Chinese screen unfolded in the far corner; a blue and white vase depicted an ornate temple and a filigree bridge beside a draping willow tree. The oriental carpet beneath her snow-dampened boots colored the floor in a dizzying array of tints and patterns. Imported goods were in high demand among the gentry and came at exorbitant cost.

"Don't you just love what they've done with this room?" Bel asked as she stood to get a closer look at the scenic wall panels. "I can almost imagine myself in Asia, staying in a charming pagoda."

"I find it frivolous. If one had traveled to the Orient and brought home mementos to remind them of their trip, I suppose I could see it."

"As you say," Belinda flounced to the door. "I'm off to the library to find a book to pass the time."

"Don't you dare leave me," Raven hissed. But her sister was already gone.

Uncharacteristically agitated, Raven stood up, turned in a circle and then sat back down. She smoothed her skirts, determining to appear outwardly poised even if her insides flipped like an organ grinder's monkey. She picked up a ceramic hut with Chinese markings from the table beside her and muttered, "Wasteful."

"They make very convincing replicas now, you know." John's amused voice caused Raven to rise and spin around. He took the statue from her gloved hands, turned it over, and pointed to a symbol printed on the bottom corner. "You see?"

Raven leaned in. A crown, surrounded with circular letters read: *Chamberlain & Co, Worchester.* She glanced back at him, unable to wash the censure from her tone. "So, you did not actually travel to Asia."

"No need." His blue-gray eyes sparkled with challenge. "I picked up this lovely trinket, on my way back from Shropshire, week before last. Chamberlain makes the highest quality ceramics. However, the one behind you is Ming Dynasty. Passed down in our family for generations."

Raven glanced at the scenic blue and white vase she'd observed earlier, noting that it appeared remarkably well preserved. She turned back to find John dipping into a low bow that somehow felt mocking.

"It is a pleasant surprise to see you, my dear," he said as he straightened, his gaze taking on a frosty cast, his normally jovial mouth pressed into a tight line. "For what do I owe the honor of your presence?"

Raven wondered for the first time if she had done irreparable harm to their relationship. Her chest constricted. She had let him down. "I'm sorry," she blurted as she took his hands in her gloved fingers and tugged him down on the sofa to sit beside her.

"For what, my dear?" His gaze held hers. He wanted her to say it.

"I apologize for missing our dinner last night. I was treating a boy at Hill House, you see..."

He stiffened and pulled his hands from hers. "How is it you are acquainted with Hill House Orphanage?"

"Peter recently became their resident physician, and I've accompanied him on several house calls there in the last weeks. Peter was at hospital yesterday when I received an urgent message that one of the boys was in respiratory distress. I had to—"

"So, you treated my brother then?"

Raven straightened her spine and searched his closed expression. Was this how he planned to tell her? How could he assume she knew who Brit was or that they'd even met? John must know more than she realized if he assumed she had made Brit's acquaintance.

Never her style to prevaricate, she replied, "Yes, I treated him for a severe apoplexy, but did not know his identity until his condition stabilized."

John gave a single nod. "How is Brit faring?"

"He will recover."

John let out a low sigh. "I put the laudanum in his tea because he was so agitated...angry even. I only wished to help him remain calm. Our appearance in his life and his newly discovered identity would be a lot for anyone to handle. But the longer we talked, the more erratic he became. He accused me of poisoning him, and then nearly strangled me before he tore out of here with the devil on his heels. After multiple inquiries by my footman, I discovered that he had returned to the orphanage. The note said he'd been treated by a doctor there and was doing well.

"I had no knowledge of your involvement before. But now it all makes sense." John ran a hand over his mouth and stared into the distance before glancing back at her. "So, you know...he has claim to my title?"

"Yes, he told me. John, I..." She swallowed another apology. Brit's return from the presumed grave could only be a blessing. John's loss of title notwithstanding, but she had to ask, "How are you, John? This must be hard for you. What will you do regarding the earldom?"

He shoved a hand through his hair. "It's quite complicated. There are entails that must be met and legal hoops to jump through. I won't bore you with all the details, my dear. But please do not worry on account of our future."

After a slight hesitation, she placed a hand on his knee. "It is quite a miracle, isn't it? Your brother alive after all these years."

"Yes." He stared down at her fingers against the dark wool of his trousers. "Thank you for saving him, Raven. There's no need to apologize for missing our dinner...or for anything at all."

Raven's heart swelled. John was a good man, and she had neglected him. Something she planned to remedy, posthaste. "Perhaps we could plan another engagement celebration?"

John did not answer right away, and in the silence, a knock sounded on the door. Two maids rushed into the parlor, one carrying an elaborate tea tray, and the other a three-tiered stand containing miniature cakes, sugar-dusted pastries, and layered finger sandwiches.

Right on time, Belinda rushed into the room behind them. "Oh, my heavens!"

"Chef Escoffier does nothing in half-measures," John said. "He's rather the best acquisition I've ever made."

Belinda sat across from them and took a long sniff of a chocolate eclair. She groaned with a roll of her eyes. "Is he considering marriage proposals?"

John dismissed the maids with a wave of his hand. Then he addressed Raven, "Now, about that engagement dinner...the servants should finish hanging the Christmas greens tomorrow. Would your family be available for Sunday supper?"

"Yes!" Bel volunteered.

Raven watched her sister with an indulgent smile. "Sunday sounds perfect."

"What of your parents?" John asked.

"I am certain they will make themselves available. As to my siblings, I will invite them, but we can proceed even if they cannot all attend."

"Will the new Lord Wexford make an appearance?" Belinda asked, her gray eyes wide and unassuming. But Raven knew better. Her sister's stark curiosity could not be more evident.

"Yes, will you invite Brit...er...Lord Wexford?" Raven asked.

Raven felt John stiffen, his voice tense. "I supposed that depends upon his health. Do you believe young Brit will be sufficiently recovered day after tomorrow?"

"I ordered bedrest for forty-eight hours." Raven's core tightened in some unidentified mix of emotions at the thought of seeing the new earl again. "If he follows my instructions, then he should feel well enough by Sunday."

Ice crunched beneath Brit's boots as he made his way across the grounds to the stable.  He passed a hedge of winter roses, their scarlet petals crystallized like glass in the snow. But his thoughts were not for the beauty of the day. He would need to acquire a few things before moving into the Wexford townhome, most urgently a travel trunk. Not that he was taking much with him. Most of his possessions would remain at Hill House, but he would need to purchase several new suits, perhaps even hire a valet. As much as he loathed the idea of another man grooming him, he was quite certain his current style of dark tweeds and trousers that he'd purchased from a used clothing stall would not do for an earl. He would need to fit in with his brothers. Become one of them.

At least in appearance.

The thought of his half brothers unfurled a deep longing in his chest. Was it possible that he'd judged them too harshly? Could he truly have a home and a family? Brothers who had mourned him all of these years? If any hope remained of repairing the delicate nature of their relationship, he would need to pursue it. And soon.

A soft ringing turned his head as a voice said, "Heard you had a nasty turn, young man."

An old man huddled in the lee of the barn. A fixture at Hill Orphanage for years, the Shadow, as the children called him, appeared little more than a vagabond with his unkempt beard, stringy, gray hair to his shoulders, and tatty clothing from a past century. Although the codger would never turn down an offer of food, he declined all invitations to enter the manse and warm himself by the fire. The previous summer, when he'd come too close and scared the younger children, Jack had threatened bodily harm if the old man didn't leave the premises. He'd disappeared for weeks, but then turned up again, keeping his distance.

Brit figured the old drifter was harmless, if a little barmy. He didn't stop to wonder how the man knew of his brush with death. He seemed to know just about everything that went on at Hill House. Brit assumed the information must be passed on by the servants along with the provisions Olivia had instructed them to give the man.

Brit tipped his hat at the hunched figure and adopted a cavalier tone. "Aye, mate. It wasn't pretty."

"You seem hale and hearty now." The man smiled warmly.

"That I am." Brit wouldn't mention the tightness deep in his chest or the fact that the world spun a bit when he turned his head.

As Brit met the man's gray eyes, a memory pierced his mind, something elusive and slippery. He stared hard, searching what little of the man's face appeared between his shaggy beard and low hat. But the mirth twinkling in his gaze wiped the familiarity away. Brit knew better than to ask if they had met. Likely in a different life, Brit had robbed the man or encountered him in some other nefarious endeavor.

"That laudanum is filthy business. I'd steer clear of it, if I were you," the old vagrant asserted, tugging Brit from the jumble of his memories.

"Of course, sir." Brit had never been one to indulge in anything that impaired his judgment. He had witnessed too many street kids fall prey to the bottle or enter an opium den never to emerge. And now, there was nothing on earth that would entice him to touch laudanum again.

A gust of frigid wind caused Brit to clamp down on his hat and the man to pull his tattered coat tighter around himself. "Why don't you come into the stable out of this harsh weather?" Brit asked the man.

"Nay, young man. I am perfectly content." His watery eyes took on a faraway look, almost as if he stared through Brit to something only he could see. "Take care, boy. Not everyone who appears a friend has your best interest at heart. Yet, one you fear to trust holds your future."

Brit rolled his eyes to the heavens. He didn't need a stranger's advice to know there were those he could not trust. But when he turned back to tell the man as much, he had vanished. Brit's gaze swept the snowy landscape. The snow a pristine sheet all around him, save for his footprints leading from the house. The old chap could not have moved fast enough to round the side of the barn, in any case. At least not by natural means.

The hair lifted on the nape of Brit's neck, and he wondered if the children's fears of the Shadow were legitimate.

Or if the aftereffects of his brush with laudanum were still affecting his brain.

With a shake of his head, he entered the barn and ordered a phaeton from the stable boy as Gillian, his favorite mare, beckoned with a whinny. "Hi there, my girl." Brit ran his hand over her velvety snout before pulling an apple from his pocket. "You know what I've got for you, eh?" The horse exposed huge teeth and nipped the fruit from Brit's palm. As a boy, he and Gillian had raced across the meadows of the Hill property, slaying imaginary dragons, and vanquishing the very real demons of abandonment and anger that had haunted his soul. He would give Gillian her head and they would fly. The faster and farther, the better. Sometimes, he would take a book and find a sunny spot on a fairy hill or beside a crystal pool and read until they lost the light. Those long, solitary afternoons had healed his broken soul.

"Sneaking off, are you?" Archie appeared beside him, seemingly out of nowhere. Brit didn't even flinch. His best friend's stealth was his trademark. When their gang had begun decorum lessons with Mrs. M, she had insisted they all choose a surname, explaining one name would never be acceptable in society. Most of the kids didn't recall their birth surnames, or if they did, they wished to distance themselves from that part of their pasts. It had been a fun afternoon debating the best name to describe each boy. Chip, with his joyful disposition and ready smile, had become Chip Lightheart. Brit had settled on Crane after a favorite fictional character. Archie's name, on account of his innate craftiness, reddish hair, and disconcerting yellow eyes, had taken all of twenty seconds for the boys to choose.

"What do you want, Fox?"

Archie leaned against Gillian's stall and crossed his arms in front of his chest. "I'm fairly certain that pretty doctor told you to stay in bed for another day."

Gillian shied away, eyes rolling. Brit leaned in to scratch behind her ear as he addressed his best friend. "That is unnecessary. I feel fine."

"Either you've been dabbling in Mrs. M's face powder again or you're lying."

"*Again*?" Brit lifted a brow. "If I recall, you were the one dousing that fiery hair in an attempt to scare the girls."

Archie nodded with a snigger. "Ah yes, they thought a ghost had come to haunt them."

Brit stiffened and Gillian nuzzled into his shoulder.

"Maryann shrieked bloody murder all the way to the MacCarrons' bedroom."

Brit chuckled despite himself.

"And Jack tanned my hide good." Archie shook his head, sobering. "Not one of my better ideas."

"Have you ever had a good one?" Brit grinned.

"Here's one, git." Archie punched Brit's shoulder. "Wherever you're off to, I'm coming with you."

Belinda looped her arm through Raven's and gushed, "Isn't it divine?"

As they strolled down New Bond Street, Raven had to agree. The thoroughfare effervesced with joy and carefree laughter. Snow piled on lampposts, and the tips of the plaza's majestic Christmas tree. Tiny pyramids of the sugary fluff topped glass ornaments and jaunty bows like frosting. Shop windows glittered with all manner of luxury merchandise, framed in verdant garlands and ribbons of scarlet and gold. A group of carolers in matching forest-green and burgundy velvet coats, each of their hats festooned with feathers, bows, and tiny silver bells, approached as they harmonized a lovely version of *God Rest Ye Merry Gentlemen*.

The light of the season suffused the air and filled Raven with hope. Her meeting with John had brought a buoyancy to her step as well. His swift pardon of her after missing the dinner he'd planned for their engagement, and his gracious acceptance of his brother's return, spoke well to his character as a gentleman. Perhaps she had merely been too distracted with her medical ambitions to open her heart to him before.

The sisters reached Alexander's Bookshop and stopped in front of the enchanting window display. Tall, wooden nutcrackers in full highland regalia stood sentinel to a fantasy scene of carved knights astride white steeds brandishing shiny lances while their porcelain ladies filled the stands with waves of rainbow-silk flags. Wind-up ballerinas in pink, tulle skirts, twirled inside wreaths of sugared plums, the tinkling tunes of their music boxes reaching through the open doorway.

"That book would be a perfect gift for Martha and the kids, would it not?" Bel pointed to a large, gilded tome of Christmas tales.

"Yes, and I'd like to..." But Raven's words trailed off as something caught her attention out of the corner of her eye. Or *someone*, more like. She turned to face two gentlemen as they approached along the walk. The shorter one, with bright hair peeking out from his top hat, sauntered beside the taller, broader gentleman moving with confident purpose.

Brit Griffin and Archie Fox.

Raven's heart galloped into her throat. Neither man had spotted her as yet, giving her a moment to steady her breath.

The pair stood out among the paunchy, over-indulged gentry like two Arabian racehorses in a field of sway-backed ponies. Brit, with his broad shoulders and ebony hair, curling slightly beneath the brim of his top hat, caused Raven's mouth to go dry. A trio of younger ladies twittered behind gloved hands, watching the young lord in a most unsuitable manner until their older chaperone scolded the girls and practically pushed them into a nearby shop.

A flutter grazed Raven's upper arm as Belinda brushed against her and followed the direction of her sister's stare.

"Oh my," Bel breathed. "How extraordinarily diverting..."

At that moment, Brit's gaze landed on Raven, and the chaos of New Bond Street went silent. Did she imagine that his steps faltered for just a beat before he set his chin and strode up to her with purpose?

"Miss Cratchit." He tipped his hat, waves of black hair falling across his forehead as he bent in a quick bow.

"Lord Wexford," Raven said, causing Bel to gasp. Raven rushed on, "How good to see you looking so well."

Bel dropped into a curtsey. When she straightened, Archie swept his hat off in a dramatic flourish, and without waiting for Raven to present her sister, said, "Mr. Archie Fox, at your service."

Belinda met Mr. Fox's gaze as if he were the answer to a whispered prayer as Mr. Fox blinked at her in obvious awe.

Raven started and stared, her gaze flitting back and forth between the two of them. Amazement bloomed in her chest as Bel replied, "I am pleased to make your acquaintance, Mr. Fox."

Raven glanced around the busy sidewalk at the merry passersby. Aside from a gentleman's annoyed frown that he was forced into the street to walk around Brit, no one paid them any mind.

Raven swiveled toward Brit to find the same astonishment she felt tugging at his mouth, his gaze flaring wide as he regarded his friend who was now bowing over Bel's fingers to kiss her gloved knuckles. But then, recovering quickly, those black eyes turned on Raven, settling on her face with direct intent. "A most prodigious happenstance, wouldn't you say, Miss Cratchit? I would say it rivals our initial encounter."

A vision from the evening in question of Brit half-clothed and gasping for breath flashed before Raven's eyes and heat rose in her skin. Desperate to distract attention from her reddening cheeks, she snapped, "What are you doing out on such a cold night? You should be in bed, sir!"

Brit's lips quirked to the side in a wicked smirk. "Is that a challenge, Miss Cratchit?"

His insinuation was not lost on her and was so far from appropriate that her hands fluttered up to tug on the muff that hung around her neck. "Well, I...you know...I instructed..."

Taking pity on her, he finished, "You instructed bedrest for two days. I am aware."

And yet, the man had completely disregarded her orders. Did he not respect her medical expertise? Or, more precisely, had he ignored her because she was a female? Years of disdain and outright ridicule from men who made it clear that a female could not possibly have the brains or fortitude for the medical profession, hardened around her. She lifted her chin. "You can ignore my advice if you like, *Lord* Wexford. But it is your life in the balance."

She had not intended to give undue emphasis to his title, but somehow, she'd known it would irk him.

Brit's eyes turned brittle as he stepped toward her. "Exactly. It is my life, Miss Cratchit."

Standing her ground, Raven crossed her arms in front of her chest and rose on her toes in an attempt to assert herself upon the giant imbecile before her. "Well, if you valued your life at all, you would have followed the orders of your doctor."

"I am not some delicate dandy who needs coddling, I assure you."

That, he was not. Grudgingly, she took in the strong arms and wide expanse of his chest, filling out a jacket that would have drowned most men. Forcing her emotions down, she commented in her most clinical tone, "Bedrest for twenty-four hours, at the very least, would have been sensible."

He arched a dark brow. "Sensible, you say? Where's the fun in that?" Their gazes locked and something sparked, like a flint kindling a flame. All that was suitable and proper flew right out of Raven's head as she drank in the fine details of his face, from the strong slash of his brows to the spikes of lashes framing eyes the color of black coffee, to a faded scar on the bridge of his nose, to the clear-cut slope of his cheekbones, and then the undeniably lovely shape of his mouth. Raven inhaled through her nose and became intoxicated with the scent of him: soap, pine trees, and open sky.

Her gaze flitted back up to meet his and suddenly she realized she and Brit stood close. *Too* close. Raven stepped back so quickly, she nearly tripped on the hem of her skirt.

To her right, Belinda asked Mr. Fox, "So *he* is the poor, lost Earl of Wexford?"

Brit, shocking Raven that he had also overheard, turned to her sister. "That, I am. But no longer lost...or poor, it would seem."

"Oh, he's lost all right," Archie commented under his breath.

From what Raven had witnessed of their decidedly unique friendship, and how they ribbed one another like siblings, the remark did not come as a surprise. But Belinda let out a throaty laugh, reminding Raven that rakes like Mr. Fox were the chink in her sister's emotional armor. And with this rake, in particular, there could be no future.

Far past time for them to retreat, Raven gave a half-curtsy. "Good to see you, Lord Wexford. I...er...we...um...must be going now!"

Brit appeared startled by their sudden departure but did not question it as he bid them adieu.

Head spinning with what had just occurred, Raven ducked into a milliner's shop, Belinda close behind. She moved through the holiday shoppers to a deserted corner and spun on her sister. "What just happened?"

Belinda's brows rose. "That man...the living embodiment of Michelangelo's David...that is the man whose life you saved, who you saw unclothed, who is the lost Ear—"

"That is not what I'm referring to and you know it!" Raven hissed and glanced around at the other women in the shop, their curious stares all swiveling in Raven's direction.

Bel propped her hands on her ample hips. "Don't change the subject."

Raven led her verbose sister to the sale racks in the back of the room where they had a semblance of privacy. "Yes," she whispered. "But his return is not our news to spread. As I told you..."

Bel crossed her arms in a pout. "It's not as if anyone would pay me any mind."

Suddenly, drained of all energy, Raven slumped against a table of assorted gloves and comforters.

"Oh...I see," Belinda breathed, eyes wide with wonder. "You have an affection for him. And really who could blame you!" She fingered a fuchsia and black lace fan with a ripped panel. "But what of John? Oh..." Her eyes widened yet again. "Everything you said was missing from your relationship, you feel with the new lord."

"No!" Raven shot to her feet and after a deep breath, tempered her voice. "Please, Bel it isn't like that. He is my patient. I saved his life. It creates a bond."

Like a dog with a bone, her sister persisted. "He was flirting with you, I saw it! But why would he do such a thing, knowing you are engaged to his brother?"

Raven glanced away, selecting a pair of silk gloves, and examining the run down each palm.

After a moment, Bel whispered into the quiet, "You did not tell him you are to marry his brother."

It wasn't a question, and Raven saw no point in denying it. "The subject did not come up."

"I see. So, as he was telling you that he is the lost earl, back from the dead, you saw no opportunity to share with him that you are betrothed to the former Earl of Wexford?"

Raven turned to a mirror and adjusted the silk lapels of her plum-colored jacket. White lace spilled out from the open neck of her coat and tickled her chin. She turned her head and assessed herself critically. Some considered her beautiful, but all Raven could see were her flaws; a too-wide mouth, full cheeks, and a short forehead. She adjusted the crown of her hat and ran a hand over the plum-colored ribbons that fell over her black hair rather becomingly. She cocked her head and wondered what Brit saw when he looked at her.

"And what happens at the engagement dinner this Sunday?" Bel asked, fluttering her lashes in a parody of flirtation. "The new Mr. Griffin appears fit. Quite toothsome in fact." She snapped her teeth together as if biting a tasty morsel.

"Belinda!" Raven spun on her sister.

"Of course, I mean to say, healthy," she clarified with an impish grin. "He is well enough to attend, wouldn't you agree?"

Her sister's words only fueled her own inappropriate feelings, so Raven pasted on a grin and gave Bel a playful push. "Enough about me. What of the charming, Mr. Fox? He appeared quite taken with you." A sudden knot formed in Raven's throat given her sister's painful history. "Unlike most, he sees you for who you truly are. Brit even..."

Belinda tossed a caramel curl over her shoulder. "Don't be daft. Such men are merely enticed by the chase. I'm quite finished with the raffish sort."

"But he sees you, Bel. He truly sees you."

Belinda frowned. "Men like that never see beyond their own ego and how a woman's presence feeds it."

Raven arched a brow, noting Bel's sudden fascination with a brown, wool gaberdine shawl. Knowing her sister's discomfort when reminded of her tragic past and current circumstance, she played along. "Is that so?"

"This shawl would do nicely for Martha, don't you think?" Bel questioned in a meek voice.

"Quite." Their older sister tended towards more serviceable clothing since having children. "May we return to our shopping, then? Christmas is less than two weeks away."

After Bel nodded her agreement, Raven turned away to hide a sigh. Her sister had accurately read her mind, per usual. Brit Griffin had most definitely captured her attention for more than one reason. Her heart gave an uncomfortable flutter. If Brit chose to claim his title, he would become a permanent fixture in her life. Her *brother-in-law*. A weight settled on her chest. How would he react when he learned the truth? Would he mind that she was engaged to John? Would the news affect him at all? The day after next, she would find out.

# Chapter Seven

*Scrooge House loomed just beyond the gate. The carriage turned a curve, and the boy released his grip, momentum flinging him across the icy pavement. He teetered dangerously. The skin of his face, previously frozen stiff, began to heat with terrible trepidation as he careened toward a drift of wintry muck. He shifted one foot behind him and dug in the heel of his boot. But instead of acting as a brake, his legs slipped out from under him, and he soared into the air.*

*The bell tolled seven…*

"I do hope you'll be comfortable here, Brit," John said. "My offer still stands to move out of the main quarters."

Brit walked over and parted the draperies of the single window, overlooking the alley and roofline of the mews. A stale scent permeated the room as if no one had set foot in it for years. But it was clean with a large four-poster, mahogany bedstead, heaped with a feather mattress, navy coverlet, and a plethora of tasseled pillows. A painting of a ship tossed in turbulent seas hung above the bed.

The handles of the wardrobe were tiny brass anchors, and a ship's wheel had been engraved on the washstand.

Brit peered into a circular mirror that resembled a porthole, noting the pale cast of his skin and dark shadows beneath his eyes. Ignoring a wave of fatigue, he turned to John. "Whose room was this?"

"Grandfather Thera stayed here when he visited. In his younger years, he captained a frigate much like that one." John nodded to the seascape.

Brit's birth records had listed his mother's maiden name as Alexandra Thera. This room had been designed for her father. *My grandfather.* Eager to learn more, he turned his attention to a painting above the hearth. Stark white windmills on a hill overlooking blue-tiled roofs and an expansive sapphire sea. He stepped closer. Something in the open sky and deep waters called to him. "Where is this?"

"Santorini. Mother's homeland."

Brit had not considered the possibility that he could have surviving relations in Greece. His mother's family. He shoved his hands into his trouser pockets to disguise his excitement as he faced John. "Are our grandparents still...there?"

John walked over to a narrow door beside the wardrobe. "No, Grandmother Thera passed when I was a baby, and Grandfather died..." He paused and tapped his chin. "Some ten years ago. Perhaps eight. I'm not certain."

"Do we have any family in Santorini?"

John's brows popped up as if he'd never considered the possibility. "I suppose. Cousins and such." He waved a hand in dismissal. "Now, this door leads..."

"You don't *know* if we have relations alive in Greece? What about here in England? Father's family?"

John opened a door to reveal another closed door on the other side and turned, his brows lowered in a scowl. "Do you mean *your* father's family?"

Brit rocked back on his heels and clenched his jaw on an angry retort. John did not have a problem owning Brit's father's title and wealth, but didn't consider himself part of the Griffin family? He stared hard at his half brother but then let out a slow breath. He'd come to Wexford House determined to start afresh. "Yes, the Griffins. I assumed since Father legally adopted you, that you would have maintained relations with them."

With a lift of his chin and a look of patient indulgence, John replied, "Ah...I see, you are searching for connections. How charming. Your father's parents died before I met them. His only sister is a spinster. Aunt Gert comes around on occasion, but she prefers to stay ensconced with her companion in Brighton." Before Brit could inquire to any cousins, John clarified, "Her *female* companion. She never had any children."

*How convenient*, Brit thought. No other male relatives meant there had been no one to contest John's inheritance of the earldom. Again, he wondered if his half brothers had thought twice about him after Father had given up the search.

"Now, tomorrow eve we will be hosting a dinner for my betrothed and her family. I will send Bert, my valet, to assess your wardrobe for the appropriate attire."

Brit crossed his arms in front of his chest. "I met with a tailor on New Bond Street today. And plan to make inquiries for my own valet. I'm all set."

John assessed Brit's tweed jacket and worn waistcoat with a missing top button. "A custom suit takes days to complete, even if you paid for a rush. I will have Bert alter something of mine for you to wear to the dinner."

"That won't be nec—"

"Surely you do not plan to wear..." He waved his hand at Brit's off-the-rack jacket that fit the breadth of Brit's shoulders but flapped loose around his waist, paired with thick, workman's trousers. "The garb of an impoverished proctor?"

Brit clenched a fist inside of his pocket. He did not like being at such a disadvantage. Admittedly, he knew next to nothing about being part of the gentry, but neither did John need to throw it in his face at every opportunity. "Thank you, I will accept Bert's assistance," he replied, fighting to keep the annoyance from his tone.

John had moved to the door but turned back before exiting. "You are staking your claim as earl, then?"

He made it sound as if Brit's title were up for debate. As if the first person to drive their flag into the ground could lay claim to the earldom. Brit straightened his shoulders and strode forward, holding John's gaze as he spoke each word with deliberation. "This is not the California gold rush, *brother*. The title has been mine since birth." He stopped when they were nose to nose, like rams battling for territory. "Do you plan to contest the will?"

John's eyes took on a hard cast, but prudently, he stepped back through the open doorway. "That would be unwise."

"Good." Brit let a bit of the tension flow out of his stance. "To answer your question, yes, I plan to claim my birthright. Mr. Veck is already working on the papers." He would not mention the marriage stipulation, but the deadline grew larger in Brit's mind with each passing hour. There had been no one who had captured his attention in ages. Not since the dalliance with Jessica, a neighboring dairy farmer's daughter, who had ended up marrying a childhood beau who had inherited a large, if run-down, estate in Hertfordshire.

No one, that is, except...a girl with a pair of fine blue-bordering–on-violet eyes.

"Then we will make the official announcement on Sunday," John stated, regaining Brit's attention. "The aristocracy will be...ecstatic with excitement at your return from the dead." Some dark emotion flickered across John's face, before he muttered, *my lord*, bowed his head, and took his leave.

Brit shut the door and walked back to the hearth. He'd engaged in territorial rows with some of the vilest thugs in London, bludgers that would give a toff like John Griffin nightmares. Yet, Brit knew this was not some backstreet brawl. The upper crust played by different rules entirely. He needed a guide, someone who could bring him up to speed quickly and help him navigate the shark-infested parlors of London's elite.

He slumped into a chair and squeezed his aching temples. Mrs. March was the only lady he knew that had any connections, but she'd been out of society so long...the dark-fringed, violet-blue eyes returned, sparking some sort of fire in his chest. Miss Raven Cratchit was brilliant, connected, and a lady he most definitely wanted to learn more about. He sat up, the decision giving him a mission, finally something he could control.

Brit *had* been feeling a bit ill, lately. Monday, he would pay a call upon the doctor.

Raven snuggled into layers of blankets as the open carriage rolled down the thoroughfare. Scents of wood smoke and roasting chestnuts curled through the air and settled on her tongue as a frosty breeze pushed back her fur-lined hood and tugged strands of dark hair across her cheeks. She adored London in winter, most especially Christmastime. The fog lifted, and the city felt poised for a fresh start, the air crisper, cleaner.

Gus clucked to the horses, and the wheels slowed as they turned onto Grosvenor Square. Twilight bathed the piazza, gilding the pine needles and junipers, sparkling with frost. Raven inhaled their perfume mixed with the tang of freshly tilled earth. An initiative to make the courtyard into a park-like setting for its residents had come earlier in the fall, just in time for the season. Only residents who lived in the square had a key to the gated area, making it a safe haven for strolls and picnics, alfresco concerts, and midnight interludes.

*Midnight interludes?* Even as she questioned the errant thought, the image of a half-shadowed face tilting down toward hers, dark waves of hair tumbling over a broad forehead as a large hand warmed her waist, sent her pulse fluttering.

What in the world was wrong with her? She was eight and ten, for heaven's sake, far past time to put away romantic fancies. Many of her friends from Ms. Goodman's Finishing School had been married for over a year. Maryann Hattburt was already a mother of two.

But as they drew nearer to her betrothed's residence, the possibility of seeing Brit Griffin—this time as his brother's fiancée—had her shoving the woolen blanket from her lap and parting her coat.

She'd dressed with extra care in one of the new gowns her mother and father had commissioned for her from Paris. Her mother had justified that she must be turned out well for her new station in life. But Raven knew Mama secretly enjoyed spoiling her girls to make up for their lack as children. And perhaps a bit of guilt over Belinda. The passing gas lamps a blur, Raven's heart squeezed. She was rarely at a loss for how to help someone. But her sister's dilemma defied logical resolutions.

With effort, Raven tugged her mind back to the present and smoothed her gown. The exquisite creation, designed to match the stones of her engagement ring, was in a modern style. The alternating peacock-blue and emerald-green panels draped and tucked around the skirt in a Grecian style, their bulk gathered in the back in a bustle. The gown tickled the edges of propriety with its fitted bodice of sapphire silk overlaid with black, and scalloped lace that made up the sheer, three-quarter-length sleeves. Belinda had voiced her jealousy that Raven wore only a few starched petticoats beneath, instead of the traditional metal crinoline.

The more tapered cut of her skirt and its flirty layers would surely turn a few heads, and perhaps ignite gossip, but Raven was no stranger to slander against her character. In her doctoring role, she'd been called everything from a harlot to a witch. She'd learned to deal with the hurtful labels by relaying them to Bel in the privacy of their home. They'd laughed themselves silly when an old dowager had pronounced, in an entirely serious tone, that clever girls die alone surrounded by cats. This, after Raven had discharged a turnip from the choking woman's throat.

But Raven did not practice medicine for adoration or even respect. She felt called to do it. Since those torturous days watching Tiny Tim suffer, and the helplessness she'd experienced as he'd wasted away before her eyes, she had known it was what she'd been born to do. Not just to assist male doctors or nurse people back to health, but to save lives. And perhaps in some small way, alter the limits placed upon her gender.

With a command from Gus, the vehicle lurched to a stop in front of the graceful four-story townhome. Every window of Wexford House glowed with gas lanterns framed by fresh pine wreaths, topped with golden bows. Festive, yet elegant. Understated.

Raven frowned as another vehicle pulled forward in front of them, the Barnacles alighting with their two young daughters. Raven's frown deepened. Clarissa and Clementine Barnacle were twins, their golden curls and dimples a thin disguise for the darkness beneath their polished exteriors. Their father, a Crimean War hero, followed his daughters and wife up the cobbled walk. Liveried servants assisted the girls along the slippery patches, their giggles giving Raven a chill that had little to do with the setting of the sun.

Belinda leaned forward and assured, "You will bring life and warmth to this place, Rave."

Raven jerked her gaze to her sister. "What?"

"Do not be rude, dear," their mother admonished from beside her on the bench seat. "Such exclamations are not ladylike."

"Let her speak as she wishes in private, Emily," Father said, angling Raven an indulgent smile.

"Well, we are about to be in a very public setting, and as the future Countess of Wexford she cannot be squawking like a costermonger when someone wishes to gain her attention." Mother lifted her chin.

Raven swallowed. She had neglected to tell her parents of Brit and his potential claim on the earldom; that, in point of fact, he was the earl by birth. Perhaps the announcement of his return had changed this intimate engagement dinner into a soiree in truth because she turned to find two more vehicles lining up behind them.

Bel beckoned Raven forward, so they leaned with their heads close. "I only meant you will infuse this household with Christmas spirit."

Raven gave a nod as Belinda rose up and then glanced behind before turning back and hissing, "Did you know the Barnacles would be in attendance? And the Tugbys and Countess Waldegrave!"

A railroad tycoon, Mr. Tugby was landed gentry like the Cratchits, but without the knighting. Countess Waldegrave had dedicated her life, and her departed husband's fortune, to building churches throughout London. They were the crème de la crème of high society.

The carriage lurched forward and then stopped at the imposing columns of the entrance. Raven caught Belinda's eye, her own nervous excitement reflected in her sister's stunned gaze. She glanced down at the heavy ring fitted over her ebony gloved finger, and then back up at her sister's sympathetic face. The presence of the elite could only mean one thing—the lost earl had returned to Wexford House.

# Chapter Eight

*The boy wiped the sticky mess of ruined stew from his shirt, flicking potatoes and hunks of beef into the snow before he forced himself to his feet. The long, narrow alley hung with fog and frost so thick the streetlamps could not penetrate it, forcing the boy, who knew every stone and shrub by heart, to grope with his hands.*

*He ventured into the darkness.*

Raven paused in the drawing room doorway, bright laughter and the chatter of a dozen simultaneous conversations creating an annoying buzz in her ears. These sorts of gatherings with their endless small talk and veiled barbs, were never her preference. She much preferred intimate dinners with family and close friends, those she could be herself around. However, she would hold her head high and play the part. These ladies and gentlemen had vast influence and could make or break her future medical practice. She touched the jeweled ornament secured at the crown of her head, patted the ringlets flowing down her back, and with chin high, stepped into the room.

"Miss Cratchit, darling!" Countess Waldegrave called as she approached, her stride bold and direct, just like the woman herself. At least sixty years of age, the countess was tall and thin, but nowhere near delicate. Her features were strong, if not attractive, and her broad smile radiated a warmth that drew one's attention to her sparkling eyes.

"My lady." Raven dropped a quick curtsy. "It's so lovely to see you."

"And you, my dear. But I must ask, what is all this about? The invitation was vague at best. Your engagement to Lord Griffin has been far from a secret. What could possibly warrant such a last-minute call of so many *élite*?"

Raven smiled, choosing to ignore the flippant reference to their social station. The countess spent most of her days, as well as her money, revitalizing places of worship and organizing fundraisers for the poor. A veiled reference to her own status could be easily forgiven.

"Lor—er—John does have quite an announcement in store, but I would be loathed to steal his thunder." As the last word left her lips, Raven spotted Brit standing alone across the room.

"Of course, darling," the countess cooed as she turned to flag down another victim for interrogation.

Brit had not yet seen her, so she indulged in a good, long stare. He had recovered remarkably. Dressed in an ebony gaberdine jacket tailored over his broad shoulders and narrow waist, paired with a crisp white shirtfront and a scarlet waistcoat that made his golden-brown skin appear to glow from within; he was quite the most beautiful human she had ever seen. A man that every girl fantasized could be real. And here he stood, holding her gaze across the crowded room.

No prevarication. No pretense. Just unadulterated admiration.

Caught in her unabashed appraisal, Raven jerked her gaze away and searched for Belinda. Where was her sister? She'd wandered off the moment the family had arrived. An exchanged nod or smile from her best friend would calm Raven's riotous emotions. But none of her siblings were in the room save Martha, who seemed fully engaged with the Barnacle twins, catching up on the latest gossip, no doubt.

With no anchor in sight, Raven's regard moved back to the man in the corner. Hands shoved in pockets, mouth tilted up on one side, he gave her a nod. As if pulled by gravity, her feet began to move. She needed to grasp hold of her professional detachment. Yes, he was attractive, but their connection was nothing more than the inevitable bond created by saving his life.

As she drew near, she noted the way his hair curled against the back of his neck, the way his broad hand gripped the top of an empty chair, his knuckles whitening as his intense gaze swept over her from head to foot. Raven felt as if no one and nothing else existed in the crowded room. A thrill traced along the exposed skin of her collarbones. This man had not been raised in drawing rooms with china teacups and polite conversation. From the little she knew of his background, that much at least was clear.

That uncultivated edge, powerful and restless like some great cat caged for viewing, only served to enhance his appeal. Her steps stuttered. Suddenly wary of his feral gaze and what it did to her, she almost turned on her heel. *He is just a man; sinew and bone;*

*blood and tissue, like every other person in the room,* she reminded herself.

Straightening her spine, she crossed the remaining distance between them.

"Miss Cratchit," Brit tipped his head to her. "If it is not inappropriate to say...you are breathtaking. And I mean that in a less than literal sense given my recent ailment." His mouth tilted, drawing out a long dimple in his left cheek.

Handsome and witty. *Lord, help her.* Raven hid her agitation by dipping into a deep curtsy. "Thank you, Lord Wexford."

As she straightened, the smile fled from his face. He lifted a hand and rubbed the back of his neck, the gesture giving him an endearing vulnerability. "Yes, I suppose that is me now. Although I do not feel the least bit lordly."

"Well, you look it." The words escaped before she could stop them.

Brit cleared his throat. "I wasn't expecting to see you here. Not that I'm complaining. Saves me from paying a call next week."

Raven lifted a brow, her medical instincts kicking in. "Are you feeling unwell? What are your symptoms?"

Humor fired in his dark eyes. "Not from my ailment. But I do have a dilemma of sorts. In fact, I have a...proposition for you."

"Oh?" To proposition a lady was the worst sort of impropriety. Yet, she could not contain her intense curiosity. She realized she'd come around the side of the chair and stood close enough to feel the heat radiating from his body.

He tilted his head down to gaze into her eyes. "You are well acquainted with my brothers, John and George, yes?"

A rock dropped into her belly. He didn't know who she was to John. Who she was soon to become to *him*—his sister by marriage. Raven took a step back, and spoke quickly before she lost her nerve, "Yes, in fact, I am engaged—"

"To me," John said over her shoulder as he encircled her upper arm in his large hand. "Raven is my beautiful bride-to-be." The words were joyous, yet his tone conveyed something darker. Pride or possessiveness?

With a delicate cough, Raven lifted her hand to cover her mouth and, in the process, tugged her arm from John's grasp. Brit's face had gone entirely blank. She had never seen anything like it. He gave no reaction outside of a slow blink. The warm, animated man who had teased her moments before was gone and in his place was a stone-faced stranger, his words perfectly cordial as he bowed his head. "Yes, we have met. Miss Cratchit is quite the physician."

His gaze slid over her, impassive.

Perhaps he was more civilized than she gave him credit for.

"She is quite brilliant, my Raven." John looped his arm behind her back and gripped her waist, anchoring her to his side. "We're going to need to channel some of that brilliance into planning our nuptials." He laughed, but Raven heard the criticism behind his words. She had simply been too busy to choose flowers and decorative ribbons and all the minor details that her mother took so much joy in arranging.

She gave a stilted chuckle. "I believe Mother has the ceremony well in hand."

"As you say, dear." John then turned to his brother. "Everyone has arrived. Are you ready to make it official, Brit?"

Those dark, fathomless eyes flicked to Raven's as he replied, "I've never been more ready."

On a raised dais, normally reserved for musicians, Brit blinked into the crowd as John cleared his throat and the room fell silent. "I've gathered my esteemed friends here this evening, those of you with the fortitude not to retreat to the countryside during these chilly months, that is."

Brit shifted on his feet as a ripple of mirth cascaded through the crowd before John continued. "I've asked you here to share a miraculous occurrence." He paused, every eye locked upon him, all signs of laughter evaporating in the web of anticipation he cast.

Brit stood at John's right with George on his other side, his life one sentence away from changing forever, and yet all he could think about was the moment when John had hovered behind Raven, gripping her arm as if she were an errant child. And worse, the obnoxious smile that had spread across his face when he'd realized he had something Brit wanted.

Brit searched the crowd and caught the glitter of sapphire crystals against sable curls but didn't dare look at her face. He clenched his teeth against the inexplicable feeling of betrayal. It was absurd. She had saved his life. Done her job. Raven Cratchit did not owe him any explanations regarding her personal life. So why then did it feel so personal that she'd left out such an important detail?

A firm hand clasped his shoulder, and John's voice boomed through the room, "My baby brother, the lost Earl of Wexford, has returned to the fold."

One could've heard a pin drop to the Persian carpet as John met Brit's gaze, his eyes brimming with tears. Brit frowned. He did not believe John's show of emotion for a heartbeat. He had enough experience with conjuring waterworks as a child—an essential weapon in an orphan's toolbox—to recognize crocodile tears when he saw them. Although he had to admire the tactic's effectiveness.

Shocked gasps evolved into whispered conjecture that snow-balled in volume until a white-haired gentleman with overgrown muttonchops demanded, "Are you the true Earl of Wexford, then?"

John's hand on Brit's shoulder tightened uncomfortably before releasing, and he answered, "Our family attorney, Mr. Veck, feels confident that Brit is the only legitimate son of Whitney and Alexandra Griffin. Which makes him the heir."

As if his name had conjured him, the little lawman appeared at the edge of the crowd, pushed his spectacles up with a finger, and gave John a satisfied nod.

A woman with graying blonde hair, dripping in jewels that made the dormant thief in Brit raise his ugly head, inquired, "Where have you been all of this time, Lord Wexford?"

Again, John jumped in. "Mrs. Barnacle, I would ask that every-one respect my brother's privacy. His life has been less than...ideal. This is quite an adjustment for him. I believe it's best to leave the past in the past."

It appeared a great kindness, and yet, Brit's hackles went up. The whole thing reeked of a setup. Brother or not, he needed to determine John's angle before it was too late.

Following the announcement, people Brit had never met rushed forward to shake his hand and welcome him home. He must have said, "thank you" perhaps a hundred times but could remember none of their well wishes, or their names.

An hour later, seated at the head of the longest table he had ever seen, Brit berated himself. The announcement had been a complete debacle. He stabbed a fork into the roast goose, silver tines striking bone. He hadn't spoken a word. Just stood there like a detached statue and let John run the show.

To his right, the woman he had escorted into dinner, Clementine Barnacle asked so many questions it was a wonder she managed to eat even a bite of the first three courses. As luck would have it, she habitually answered her own inquiries, requiring him only to grunt and nod occasionally.

As the fourth course was cleared away, Miss Barnacle leaned over and whispered, "Were you homeless then? That's quite the worst thing I could possibly imagine. Alone in the world with no family or possessions." She shuddered, took a sip of the crimson wine that had been refreshed continually throughout the meal, and then set down the crystal goblet, her gloved fingers brushing against his where his hand rested on the linen cloth. "My goodness, your hands look so strong."

Brit shifted and moved his hand away from hers. But she did not appear to notice as she launched into her next set of theories.

"Did you work on the docks? No, your skin is too nice. It must have been a workhouse!"

Thankfully, Brit had never set foot in a workhouse. Too many chaps entered those torture chambers lured by warmth and food, never to see the sun again. But he nodded all the same and glanced down the length of the table to where Raven sat between George and John, her parents directly across from them chatting amiably with their future son-in-law. Brit wondered if John's loss of title influenced their opinion of him at all. By their open smiles, it didn't appear so.

The woman to his left, a stately-looking countess, took pity on him and attempted to redirect Miss Barnacle's singular attention with topics of charity. So as the dessert course was placed before them, Brit took a bite of the sunny, lemon cheesecake and contemplated the rock that had settled uneasily in his gut. More than the heavy, French food he'd consumed, the tangle of emotion made him jittery and restless to run. He realized his right leg vibrated an agitated rhythm beneath the table. He forced his foot flat to the floor and shoved another bite of cake into his gullet. He needed to get a grip. Olivia, one of his mentors and protectors since childhood, had always said that the first rule to survival was not to give in to emotion. *Lose control and you're dead.*

Although this wasn't the street, it was just as cutthroat, and he had to believe the same rule applied.

He glanced up to find Raven's eyes on him. Through the wavering candle flame, it appeared that a tiny frown wrinkled her perfect forehead, her eyes soft. He knew that look, had seen it throughout his childhood and used it to his advantage. *Pity.* Something dark bloomed in his chest. For reasons only she knew, she had chosen to keep her engagement to his blasted brother a secret.

The day she'd saved his life, when he'd confessed his true identity to her, she had not mentioned it. Nor when they'd met on New Bond Street. Nor this evening when she had flirted shamelessly with him moments before John had approached. Clearly, he did not understand highbrow ladies' behavior. Perhaps the fire she enjoyed kindling between them was all part of the game.

Regardless of her motivations, Brit was now left with no allies in a foreign world of dinner parties and politics that he knew next to nothing about. He needed a plan.

There were many young ladies in attendance whom he could court. Those who could guide him through the maze of polite society. In fact, with his newfound wealth, he could likely have his pick. Raven Cratchit could be replaced.

He took another bite of the tart cake and began to feel better. Perhaps Bert the valet could assist him in some instruction. Or at least point him toward a book he could read on the topic. *How To Become an Earl in Ten Days.* Or something like, *Street Rat to Landed Gentleman, an Instruction Manual.*

He swallowed a chuckle as he envisioned what Chip would have to say about such a quandary. Likely, he would bluff his way through it, and quite successfully. No matter how fearful or angry, that boy could turn on the charm like a switch, beguiling even the most crotchety into his favor. And Jack...Jack MacCarron would make a move that left little doubt as to who was in charge.

Brit observed the table, and seeing that most everyone had finished their meal, decided on a course of action that would combine both strategies. He put his napkin on his plate, stood, and pasted a broad smile on his face. The clinking China and chatter quieted instantly.

"This has been a lovely, if not overindulgent feast." Brit patted his full abdomen, drawing agreement and laughter from many. "I would like to thank each of you for being here to celebrate my return and..." He raised his glass to Raven Cratchit as he said, "My brother, John's engagement."

Glasses clinked together along with cries of, "Here, here!"

Raven did not move, only watched him with wide eyes.

Brit tore his gaze away from her and addressed the table at large, "I would like to invite the gentlemen to join me in the billiard room. I believe George has arranged for a variety of after-dinner cigars." He caught his half brother's gaze with a slight raise of his brow. In point of fact, George had quite the extensive smoking collection, that Brit had gathered he only shared with a chosen few. But in the face of Brit's generosity, George would not have occasion to deny the offer.

George rose from his seat with a strained smile. "Yes, quite right. Smoking jackets will be made available as well."

As the room broke up, the women formed little groups and headed to the drawing room for coffee. Brit caught John's eye. Intense and assessing, he did not break the stare and neither did Brit. Finally, his eyes narrowing, John tipped his head in a barely discernable nod. Well versed in nonverbal male challenge, Brit interpreted the gesture without words.

*Game on, brother.*

# Chapter Nine

*Scrooge House was old and dreary, for nobody lived in it but Scrooge, save a long-standing caretaker couple and the boy, who did not relish being kicked out of the first building he had memory of living in. He approached the portico, a ferocious dread curdling his stomach.*

*The door creaked open...*

If gossip could be measured on a temperature scale, the Griffins' drawing room had reached a blistering fever. A harpist played divine renditions of Christmas carols in the corner, her lyrical notes drowned out by the ebb and flow of female voices.

An obsession had ignited.

Raven moved from group to group, introducing topics from fashion to the weather. Outside of several questions concerning her new gown, the conversation invariably circled back to the young earl's return from the dead. Not that she could blame them. The fine figure he presented, combined with the mystery of his background, was quite delicious. But the hubbub only served to fuel her own preoccupation. What had he meant by 'a bit of a proposition?' What sort of proposition?

She stopped in a group of ladies that included her older sister, Martha, and Clementine Barnacle, who questioned, "Why does he use the name, Brit? Surely that is not his Christian name?"

"No, I believe it was Bartholomew..." Martha, always up on the latest social intrigue, replied.

"Whitney Rhys Griffin," Lady Gilbert said with a sigh. The pretty, red-haired woman had been widowed two years ago, her husband leaving her with a minor title, a fortune, and six children. An infamous flirt, it was rumored Lady Gilbert had a penchant for younger men.

"Pardon?" Martha asked.

"His full name is Bartholomew Whitney Rhys Griffin, after his deceased father," the widow clarified.

"Then why Brit?" Clementine's pert nose wrinkled. "It's so...pedestrian."

"It suits him." Raven hadn't meant to speak aloud. But it was true. It was a strong, solid name.

"Oh, Raven!" Clementine spun toward her, and after giving her gown a disdainful once-over, clearly preferring the pale fabrics that maidens were expected to wear, even if those shades washed out her wan complexion, said, "You must have the inside track, being almost related to the man."

Raven clenched her fist to keep the grimace from her face.

"Yes," Lady Gilbert said, turning to Raven. "Is it true what they say?"

"*They* say quite a lot." Raven quirked a brow. "To which outrageous rumor are you referring?"

Lady Gilbert's eyes sparkled. "That he was born deformed, and his parents sent him to a remote island in the Mediterranean to live with his poor relations, of course."

"Clearly, he is not deformed." Martha rolled her eyes.

Clementine waggled her brows. "That we can see…"

Raven had seen quite enough to know the man had been formed in something close to perfection. Feeling her face heat as the group broke into giggles, she slipped away.

With a glance over her shoulder to make sure she wasn't observed, she exited the room and turned down a dark hallway, intent upon a washroom hidden deeper in the house. She needed some time alone to think. Her parents, as she knew they would be, had seemed fine with John's loss of title. Although her father did grill him a bit regarding "the manner in which he planned to keep his daughter." John had reassured them all that he had wisely invested the inheritance from his biological father. At a young age, the family attorney, Mr. Veck had advised him to keep that money in a separate account. So even if Brit booted him into the street, which John did not imagine happening, he had his own estate holdings and a substantial fortune. Which seemed to satisfy her father.

All during dinner, Raven couldn't shake a feeling of claustrophobia. In fact, when John had laid a heavy hand on her leg beneath the table linen, she'd had to focus all her attention on drawing breath. His gesture could be construed as improper despite their betrothal. Not that she'd ever been a stickler for the rules, but it had made her feel decidedly uncomfortable.

The discussion had turned to the banns being read the next morning at church—the first of three weeks of announcements that would solidify their engagement in the eyes of society. Banns were rarely done with the aristocracy. John had offered to pay for the special marriage license, which would negate the need for the clergyman to make the series of announcements, but her mother had insisted that some customs were meant for a purpose.

Not once had they asked her if *she* wished to have the banns read or if she wanted to take a month-long wedding trip to Paris after the ceremony. Which she certainly did not. Who would check in on the kids at the Ragged School or the Hill Orphanage? Peter couldn't keep up with all their patients *and* do rounds at the hospital. The banns she could do nothing about, but she resolved to speak to John about the wedding trip at first opportunity.

What she could not surmise was what had changed between her and John. Admittedly, the marriage was not a love match, but she cared for him. Admired him. She had felt sure when she accepted his proposal that the affection she felt could sustain them and grow into something more. He was quite perfect for her in every way. Handsome. Well-connected. Generous. And indulgent of her unorthodox career. But as the wedding date drew nearer, the closer he...hovered.

He'd made a comment during dinner about her "hobby" as a doctor. Something she'd never heard him say before. But the word had caused her chest to squeeze uncomfortably.

Raven felt her way along the dim corridor and turned right, slamming into a solid mass. She let out a breathless yelp as she stumbled back, and the shadow figure took her by the arms, steadying her on her feet.

Her gaze jerked up, the outline of the man unmistakable. "Brit?"

"Aye. My apologies."

Unnerved by his close proximity, she snapped, "What are you doing skulking around back here?"

"Skulking, you say?" he quipped. "That would imply evil intent, but I assure you I'm doing more dodging than skulking."

"Well, whatever you are doing, you nearly frightened me to death," Raven huffed, her pulse still pounding in her ears.

"Can't have that now, can we?" The deep timbre of his voice did nothing to help the sparks skittering along her skin as his warm fingers brushed the side of her neck.

She pulled away from his touch. "What is that supposed to mean?" Her eyes adjusted to the gloom, and she could make out the whites of his eyes and the flash of strong teeth.

He stepped back, leaned a shoulder against the wall and slipped his hands into his trouser pockets. "Merely that my elder brother may not take kindly to harm coming to his precious princess."

"His princess?" Raven crossed her arms beneath her chest. "What nonsense!"

"You are his beautiful bride-to-be, are you not?"

Her eyes adjusted further, and by the mild smirk on his mouth she could tell he'd thrown John's words back at her on purpose. "We are betrothed, yes, but I am nobody's princess."

People had been underestimating her, treating her like a delicate flower, most of her life. But despite the way she may appear, there was nothing fragile about her. She was not some dull-witted ninny, whose greatest ambition involved whom to marry. She lifted her chin, and able to make out the planes of his face in the dark, met his gaze. "I am my own person."

"Glad to hear it." His grin widened as he removed his right hand from his pocket and opened it, palm up. A silver chain connected to a heart sat coiled against his olive skin.

Raven's hand flew up to her neck to find the locket John had given her for their engagement, gone.

"Don't allow him to force you into a mold, Raven. You have a calling bigger than being a man's possession."

Something lodged in her throat as she stared at the locket, still resting in his outstretched hand. No one. Not even her family members, who loved her most of all, had ever spoken such words to her; given such importance to her career.

Raven's eyes lifted again to his and to her utter mortification she felt the sting of tears clinging to her lashes. She lowered her head and blinked them away. Then ever so slowly, she reached out, scooped the necklace from his palm, and whispered, "Thank you…"

Brit gave a single nod. Silence stretched between them, but Raven, feeling the tug of that infernal gravity, wasn't quite ready to let the encounter end. "How did you do that? Take the necklace without me knowing?"

He shrugged a broad shoulder. "It's a useful skill I learned as a child. The keys are picking the right mark and determining the best distraction."

Remembering his fingers on her skin, she teased, "Oh? Did you often use flirtation as a distraction?"

He held her gaze, a myriad of unreadable thoughts churning in his eyes. "Whatever means necessary."

After an extended moment, he broke the stare and glanced at the chain dangling between her fingers. "It also helps to choose something that won't be missed until you've escaped or handed it off to your mate."

A smile of amazement tugged at her lips. "You are the most improper gentleman I've ever met." The words, meant as an affront, came out in a breathless whisper that was anything but an insult.

"Maybe that's because I'm not a gentleman."

He'd stated a fact. But if he wasn't a gentleman, what was he? Where had this man come from? What in his past had shaped his unconventional views? And unusual skills...

A wild, reckless notion took hold of her, and she stepped forward, closing the distance between them. A gentleman would back away. Reject her advances. Brit didn't move a muscle but kept his shoulder against the wall as she clutched the fabric of his jacket and looked up into his face. "That's not a bad thing, Brit Griffin. Please don't ever change."

He searched her face, his eyes heavy and dark. Warmth flooded Raven from head to toe as he leaned toward her. Her lips tingled in anticipation, and she rose on her toes, aligning her mouth with his.

Laughter sounded behind them. Raven jerked back and spun around. No one had seen them, but female voices were growing louder just around the corner. She turned back to Brit, "I have to go..."

The hallway was empty. Making her wonder for a heartbeat if she'd imagined the entire encounter—their almost kiss.

The sound of the giggling ladies moved farther away. Visitors likely lost in Griffin Manor's maze of corridors. Raven slumped back against the wall and clutched the locket in her hand. She attempted to summon the appropriate guilt for her actions but only regretted that she had not had the opportunity to ask him about his earlier mention of a proposition.

Taking several deep breaths, she worked to get her pulse back to a normal pace and then clasped the necklace back around her neck. Perhaps she and Bel were more alike than she had realized.

Brit hung back and watched the remaining guests gather their belongings. The two-story entryway echoed with their heels tapping on the parquet floor as farewells were said. Brit watched but didn't engage. He'd had enough social interaction for the night, perhaps the next month, although he surmised this dinner was just the beginning of his societal obligations as earl. Which brought him back to his original dilemma—he had no clue how to be one. His gaze skipped over the crowd to the ebony-haired girl standing beside John. As his brother lifted her sable-trimmed wrap onto her shoulders, those vivid eyes met Brit's and his mouth went dry, his palms damp. Keats had been right, it turned out; touch did have a memory.

He swallowed and shifted his gaze, only to have it land on John who stared at him, hard. Brit shuttered his expression and slid his hands into his pockets, fighting off a wave of guilt. He didn't regret what he'd said to Raven, but he knew he needed to quell the attraction between them.

Alas, he'd always enjoyed playing with fire.

The blonde miss who'd sat next to him during dinner appeared wrapped in snow-white fur. "T'was a pleasure meeting you, my lord." She dipped into a curtsy, curls bouncing. That's when he noticed the softness of her jaw. This was the other twin, Clarissa.

Brit's brows gathered as he searched for the appropriate response that wasn't a blatant lie. Coming up empty, he replied, "And you, Miss Barnacle."

"I do hope our paths will cross again soon." Clarissa leaned toward him and lowered her voice. "Mother plans to invite you to our Christmas musicale next week. Clementine is a master of the pianoforte and I've been told I have the voice of an angel. Invites are coveted."

"I imagine so." Brit clamped down a laugh at the image of the sisters doing anything at all angelic but could not stop an ironic grin, that unfortunately, Miss Barnacle took as encouragement. She then launched into a diatribe on the superiority of her and her twin sister's skills over other holiday performances of the gentry.

Brit's mind had begun to wander when Clementine Barnacle rushed into the foyer, face white and eyes wide.

Well acquainted with the signs of physical panic, Brit's posture went rigid, and he took in his surroundings, searching for the threat as he reached for a weapon he did not have.

The girl's hushed, but flustered voice carried through the space. "Father. It's missing...just gone. I've looked everywhere."

"What's missing, dear heart?" Mr. Barnacle asked with an indulgent smile.

The room had gone silent as the girl struggled through tears, "My diamond bracelet. The one Grandmama gave me. It's been stolen."

"Someone call the authorities!" Mrs. Barnacle squawked.

Gasps reverberated through the room, with good reason. The thief in Brit had noted the piece of jewelry on Clemintine Barnacle's wrist during dinner. He estimated it contained five carats of diamonds, valued at hundreds, if not thousands, of pounds, and her sister wore an identical bauble.

The butler, Grant, exchanged a look with John and then fled down a back corridor.

The guests shifted uncomfortably, and quiet speculation descended. As Brit scanned the room for possible culprits, John's gaze flew to his, a muscle flexing in his jaw. Every person in the room followed that glower until they all turned to stare at Brit, hurtling him back in time to his years on the street; the distrust when toffs saw his ripped clothes and dirty face. Assuming his guilt without evidence. A street rat; dishonorable. *Unworthy.*

Searching for a light in the storm, Brit found Raven. She blinked at him with wide eyes as she clutched the locket at her throat. The necklace he'd stolen from her not two hours prior. Sweat broke out beneath his collar, and he fought the urge to run or voice a denial. But he remained silent, knowing such an argument would only solidify his guilt.

The silence stretched into a physical thing, crackling in the air.

Bob Cratchit stepped into the middle of the room, short and round with kind blue eyes, his voice rang with a surprising air of authority. "What is it I'm missing here? A valuable disappeared. An investigation should be launched, beginning with the servants."

"Quite right," George agreed, shooting John a narrow-eyed glare. "There's no need for anyone to panic and begin throwing around accusations."

John's suspicion of Brit had been clear to everyone present. Even if only he and George knew of Brit's past life as a thief. Although Raven also, must have an idea after he'd so foolishly revealed his nefarious skill to her.

Brit reminded himself that he had done nothing wrong and gave a nod to George. Then, he squared his shoulders, faced the room, and spoke out, "Indeed, we will be sure to call a constable in the morning. I want to thank all of you for attending this evening to support my *coming out*, as it were."

Everyone laughed, perhaps a bit too heartily, at Brit's joke. A girl's "come out" when she took her place in adult society as marriageable was quite a serious endeavor. Or so he'd heard. But the jest did the trick and conversation resumed as coats and muffs were secured.

John's mouth set in a tight smile as he said his goodbyes to each party, last of all to Raven and the Cratchits. Raven ignored Brit as she fled from the house. Her sister glanced at him, her gaze shrewd, but unreadable.

Brit hung back, clenching his jaw. Biding his time.

As the door snapped shut, John turned to face him. "If you required funds, you only needed ask."

"So, that's it then?" Brit ground out. "You just assume I took it?"

"Well, who else—"

"Who else, what?" Brit cut him off, stalking forward. "Has a background as a pickpocket? An orphan thieving to survive?"

"Some things become a habit." John shrugged. "A compulsion."

Brit's muscles quivered as he squeezed his hands into fists, his next words spoken with careful control. "I did not take it. I own everything in this bloody house and a fortune besides."

"Not yet, you don't." John leaned forward until they were nose to nose.

George stepped up and pushed a hand on each of their chests. "Let's cool down. Have a brandy in the library."

John leaned back and crossed his arms, a smirk tilting his mouth. "Mr. Veck told me of the marriage stipulation. You forfeit all of it if you don't take a bride by Christmas. Perhaps you were tucking a little away as insurance?"

The tension left Brit's shoulders and for the first time he wondered if Mr. Veck had a conflict of interest in representing both parties in the estate. But that didn't explain John's contradictory behavior. "Then why announce me as the earl?"

"It was the right thing to do."

Brit's brows lifted. "Was it also the right thing to do to make it clear to every person in this room that you thought I stole that blasted bracelet? Because your face said it all."

"He's right, John," George said. "You know those busybody twins will have the news spread from Blackfriars to Kensington by mid-morning tea."

Brit shoved a hand through his hair, the tailored fit of his suit restricting the movement. He fought the urge to flee to Hill House and sleep in his own bed surrounded by his books and the comfort of friends. Instead, he leveled his gaze on John. "Besmirch my character again and you'll have an all-out war on your hands. I do not believe you want that, *brother*."

A loud series of knocks sounded on the front door and John smirked. "I most certainly do not. Nor do I plan to fight for anything that I already own."

Grant flung open the door to admit two glowering constables, cheeks red and likely unhappy they had been called out on such a cold night.

Brit's heart stopped and then sped out of control. All these years later, and the sight of that starched uniform, metal buttons, and tall blue hats still struck terror in his chest.

John's smile widened on Brit. "This is not some street fight, Brit. But as you wish, I will play as if it is one."

Brit took two steps back as the coppers advanced into the foyer, hands gripping holstered truncheons—a weapon Brit had felt the sting of more than once in his young life.

"This man stole a diamond bracelet worth three thousand pounds." John swung an accusing finger toward Brit. "Arrest him!"

# Chapter Ten

*S*crooge *stared hard and sharp as flint. The cold within him froze his old features, shriveled his cheeks, and made his lips blue as he inquired in a grating voice, "Where is it?"*

*The boy took a step back and wrung his hat in a death grip. "I slipped, sir. On the ice. But I can get more!"*

*The old man stepped forward with such evil about his countenance that the boy stood immobilized, even as Scrooge raised his open hand.*

*The boy shrank back.*

A nasty wind swept in from the sea, nipping at Raven's exposed nose and burning her ears despite the hood covering her head. She pushed her feet faster, gripping the handle of her doctor's bag like a security blanket.

Golden Square, once an esteemed area for gentry and politicians, had gone down in the world, its great estates broken up into rooms for rented lodgings. Raven had volunteered to make two house calls in the area and had declined a comfortable carriage ride in favor of walking.

She considered herself a fair judge of character. It was she who always sniffed out the addicts who faked their pain to gain opium. She, who had sensed Lord Eaton's true nature before he'd cheated on Bel. She, who had met a potential investor in her father's business and discerned his unsavory intentions. Observation of details that others looked past was one of her strengths as a physician. There were always tells—fidgeting, evading eye contact, excessive lip licking, halting dialogue. Those observations followed by a few well-aimed questions seemed to ferret out one's true intentions.

And yet, Brit had exhibited none of it.

The plinking notes of a piano from a lower-level room, a harp from down the street, and a set of violins through a third-floor window, floated in discordant harmony through the air. Many musicians who played for the opera and theater resided in Golden Square. It was a colorful area known for its artists and foreigners. A dark-complexioned man with bushy whiskers and gold in his ears, approached and tipped a carrot-colored bowler hat to her. She gave a smile and a nod in return. They were a friendly lot here, living on the inspiration of their creative minds.

Raven had almost reached her destination at number thirty-five but slowed her steps. The semi-circle of buildings had cut down the wind and a fleeting bit of sunshine peeked through the clouds. Needing a moment before attending to the colicky baby she could already hear wailing in the distance, she approached a bench that faced the park square and sat across from the half-naked statue of an unnamed king, his rounded belly protruding over a loosely wrapped toga. She pushed back the fur of her hood and lifted her face to the sun.

Behind her closed eyes, a dark, midnight gaze leveled upon her; unwavering. But the evidence, that only she knew, was damning:

One: Brit had stolen her locket from around her neck without giving her the slightest hint that he had done so.

Two: He admitted to the skill of thievery.

Three: John's accusing glare aimed at Brit the moment he'd heard Clementine's bracelet had been stolen.

That gut reaction had been unguarded and unequivocal, which led Raven to wonder what John knew of Brit's past that she did not. Under the heat of John's stare, Brit had melted a bit. His shoulders had slumped as his gaze rushed to meet hers. Was he afraid she would tell everyone what had transpired between them in the darkened hallway?

She shivered. Not likely.

"Penny for your thoughts." Bel appeared on the bench beside her; a shimmery outline that filled in like paint spreading through water.

"Where have you been?" Raven questioned more accusingly than she'd meant to. Her sister had quite literally disappeared before entering Wexford House. Most times when Belinda disappeared, Raven harbored the secret hope that her sister had made peace with this life and moved on. But selfishly, she'd needed her best friend at that horrendous Griffin dinner party and subsequent fallout.

"Around. I had some thinking to do," Bel said as she smoothed the silk of her peach and mauve skirt. The dress she'd worn for the past two years. The dress she'd died in.

Raven clenched her teeth and squeezed her eyes closed against the clang of memories pounding in her head. A splash of dawn light across pallid skin, the lifeless stare, white tablets dotting scarlet linen. A hastily scrawled note that confirmed the catalyst for her sister's rash actions. Belinda had taken her own vibrant, precious life over a man.

As if Raven needed any further proof of the perils of love. She straightened her shoulders and lifted her medical bag onto her lap. But the action didn't stop the warning bell from ringing. Brit held the same danger for her—uncontrolled and vulnerable feelings that could jeopardize everything. She—Raven the Reliable, the Stoic, the Sensible—held the same capacity to drown in her devotion, suffocated by unfathomable emotion.

Everyone believed her detached, and perhaps a bit cold. Only Bel knew that Raven's

scope of feeling was as wide and deep as the ocean—a dangerous precipice that once crossed would consume her. Precisely like her sister. Thus, Raven would not—could not—give in to the powerful sentiment.

"Rave?" A flutter of butterfly wings brushed against her fisted fingers.

Raven took her beautiful sister's hand, marveling at her corporal presence even after all this time. "I hoped you'd gone this time," she whispered, the lie catching in her throat and burning her eyes.

A sad smile flitted across Bel's face. "You know I wouldn't...*go* without saying goodbye to you."

Raven stared down at the scuffed toes of her boots, disgusted by her selfishness. Who was she to deny her sister eternal peace? Of course, she wished her sister would move on.

"Besides, how can I leave behind all of this excitement? The lost Earl of Wexford returned and handsome as sin!"

"And about as treacherous," Raven muttered before clearing her throat and asking, "Did you hear about the stolen bracelet?"

"I did. But you cannot think Brit Griffin actually took it?"

"I'm not so sure. What do we really know about his past? Where he's been all of these years?"

Bel pulled her bottom lip into her mouth.

Raven swiveled to face her sister. "What aren't you telling me?"

"Just that we shouldn't judge a person without knowing all the facts." Hastily changing the subject, Belinda asked, "How did Brit react when he found out you are engaged to his brother?"

Brit's empty expression had said all that he did not. Heat infused Raven's neck as she thought about how she'd behaved when they'd met in the darkened corridor. She'd practically thrown herself into his arms and he had merely stood there watching her make a ninny of herself! "I don't believe he cares a whit. Besides, John is the reasonable match for me."

"Reasonable?" Bel's brows winged up.

"Perfect," Raven clarified with a decisive nod.

"But Brit Griffin can see me, can he not?"

Raven nodded, still marveling at the oddity. She'd been so wrapped up in her attraction to him that she had forgotten to ask him how such a thing was possible. Or perhaps it was more that she did not know how to broach the subject that they were each living with the spirit of someone who had passed on. This was not a conversation one approached lightly. *By the by, I noticed your friend Mr. Fox is among the unliving. How do you find such a relationship?*

"He is the first one who has seen me, besides you," Bel said softly.

"It would seem so," Raven murmured as a gentleman approached with a long black beard and a bit of round fabric perched on the back of his head, a yarmulke. He carried an enormous instrument case in a bell-like shape. Raven presumed it contained some sort of horn. A large group of eastern European Jewish families occupied a corner of Golden Square, although they, as yet, were resistant to medical treatment from outsiders such as Peter and herself.

After the man had rushed past without so much as a nod, Raven asked her sister, "And what do you know of Mr. Fox?"

Bel grew still, her aura flickering as she gazed into the sky, a patch of brilliant blue eclipsed between shifting clouds. "His is not my story to tell."

A careening cry pierced the quiet of the square, the baby's wail followed by a shout. Raven shot to her feet. "Well, that's my cue. Are you coming?"

Belinda shook her head, curls brushing her shoulders as she faded. "I have something I must d..."

But before she had finished speaking, Bel winked out of existence.

Raven started and blinked at the empty spot beside her. From what she had observed, Belinda went where her heart called her. Since they had been the best of friends in life, that often meant she appeared at Raven's side. Although Bel did occasionally shadow their parents or one of their siblings when they were in a time of high emotion—even if they did not see or feel her presence.

Raven could only hope Belinda's sudden disappearance did not mean a family member was in distress.

Belinda, no longer held back by the constraints of society, nor corporeal limitations for that matter, appeared at Archie Fox's closed bedroom door in the attic of Hill Orphanage. Once her heart had decided to speak to him, her body had followed. She could have willed herself inside of his room but had found out the hard way during her time as a spirit, that startling the living—or even the dead in this case—never turned out well.

Bel stared at the door, smoothed her hair and then her skirt and worked to calm her breathing. This highly irregular visit must be done. She could see no other way to keep her bullheaded sister from ruining her life.

Since her poverty-stricken childhood, Belinda had had one purpose in the world: to protect her family. She had ensured, as best she could with her limited resources, that they were happy and well cared for. She had dedicated herself to inventing new games that would occupy her siblings on cold winter evenings and distract them from the hunger pangs that had plagued them all. She had lost count of the times she'd given up her meager dinner to Tiny Tim or sat up with him during the night when he was in too much pain to sleep. Yet, she had failed her baby brother time and again; none of her efforts making a bit of difference. Thankfully, Mother and Father's relentless love and perseverance had prevailed—with a bit of help from Mr. Scrooge's influence and fortune.

Bel could not blame her parents for their singular focus even if their preoccupation with Tim's health had meant they had less attention to give to their other, hale and hearty, children. Thus, they sometimes missed the struggles they had each endured.

Lucy Ann most of all.

*Raven*, Bel corrected herself.

The name Lucy had never fit her younger sister, who had liked to dissect the dead creatures that their housecat dropped at her feet. Raven's brain had always worked differently. More logical with less fancifulness. As a child, Raven had followed in Peter's footsteps and shunned romantic fairytales in favor of texts on the cellular makeup of human beings or the most recent medical remedies.

Yet, it would seem, the ruling paradigm of poverty solidified one's view of life; even after money and material possessions were plentiful. Therefore, Belinda never stopped trying to protect her loved ones, even after they no longer needed her—or thought they didn't.

When the Cratchits had the funding to send the girls to a finishing school, Raven's first year had been a misery. Even at the age of twelve, she was precocious enough to question her instructors on the chemical reactions used to create the perfect patisserie and had pushed for more useful lessons than singing and needlepoint technique in favor of mathematics and science. She was wholly ignored by her teachers and an object of ridicule to the other students. Raven's pale skin, stark black hair, undernourished, angular body, and too-serious mien did not help.

Once, after school when Raven did not appear for them to walk home together, Bel had found her sister locked in a basement closet with a black eye and a bloody lip. Her views on the impracticality of learning to serve a proper tea had proved to be one too many condescending judgments, and her fellow classmates had turned on her like a rabid pack of wolves.

That day began a sort of transformation in Raven, who had finally seen the evidence that her actions were odd and her logical conclusions sometimes hurtful to others. She cared for others' feelings, perhaps a bit too deeply, so had learned to turn off the erudite parts of her brilliant brain in order to survive in the environment of privilege she'd found herself in. Subsequently, once she began to pay attention to her toilette and ate enough to put a bit of meat on her bones, Raven had transformed into a great beauty.

Looks, it seemed, allowed others to forgive a myriad of eccentricities. Even John Griffin had looked past Raven's lack of pedigree and her chosen profession when he had offered for her hand. But from what Bel had witnessed, John did not plan to allow Raven to continue her pursuit of medicine once they were married. And anyone with eyes could see Raven did not love the man. She'd admitted as much herself.

But there was one she did love.

Belinda raised her arm to knock just as a hand reached through the door and pulled her bodily through the wood.

# Chapter Eleven

*H*and raised, Scrooge spat, *"What right have you to lose my dinner? The man who pays you, feeds you, clothes you!"*

*The boy stood still and did not run. He would rather take a beating and let the old man get it out of his system.*

*As if reading the boy's fears, Scrooge lowered his fist and growled, "But no more."*

*"Please, sir!" The boy rushed up to grasp Scrooge's rail-thin arm. "Don't put me out. Tis Christmas Eve!"*

*"Christmas?" Scrooge spat. "Bah, Humbug!"*

"Bloomin' hell, Brit," Jack McCarron muttered as they ducked out of the police station into the harsh morning light. "All those years on the streets you managed to avoid the coppers. Two days as a gentleman and I'm bailing you out of the clink."

"I'm bloody well aware," Brit snapped.

As much as Brit loathed to disappoint the man who was like a father to him, the night he'd just spent trapped in a cell with drunks and vagrants—his fancy suit painting a fat target on his back—had frayed his nerves. He'd been forced to punch out a bludger who had attempted to peel the jacket from Brit's very shoulders, and afterwards, had slumped against the wall not daring to close his eyes the entire night. And if that were not enough, he now had to deal with the repercussions of his blasted brother framing him for theft in front of the very gentry he was trying so hard to fit in with.

Not to mention the negative impression he must have made on the Cratchits. Not that he should care.

"Will the family press charges against you?" Jack asked.

"I don't see how. I didn't take the blasted bracelet." Brit sighed. "But I thought about it."

Jack gave a nod of understanding. Once a thief, always a thief.

Brit jammed a hand through his tousled hair and spat, "I don't know the rules, Jack. On the streets, there was a code of sorts—toolers watched out for toolers, work your own territory, avoided the magistrate, and stay alive. Turns out, toffs don't play fair."

"I could have told you that." Jack chuckled. "You should've seen the way Topher used to treat me. If that git had been smart enough to set me up, I wouldn't be here now."

Christopher March was Lois's nephew. The rivalry between Jack and Topher, after Lois took Jack under her wing, was legendary. Yet, somehow, they had ended up the best of friends. "How did you do it?" Brit asked as the carriage pulled up, and Roger jumped down to open the cab door.

"Win over Topher March?" Jack asked as he climbed in.

"Yes," Brit clarified, taking a seat on the leather bench, opposite Jack.

"That's a long story." Jack sighed, then said to the driver, "Wexford House, Roger."

"No," Brit shook his head. "The orphanage first. I need to get my feet under me."

"Which is what John Griffin will expect you to do...turn tail and hide while he sits like a king inside of *your* house." Jack cocked a brow.

Street rules would also dictate that possession equaled ownership. *Your score, your prize.* Growing up, his little gang of misfit thieves had fought hard to keep their hideouts over the years, even going so far as to use secret passwords for entry and rigging traps to keep out the riffraff.

"Which is it then, mates," Roger asked as a shout sounded, and the startled team jerked the carriage forward a pace. "We're blockin' traffic."

Brit may possess the legal right to his father's ancestral home, but John Griffin was still treating it like his territory and defending it as such. The question was, how could Brit stake his claim without John thwarting him at every turn? First the laudanum, followed by a setup that had led to Brit's arrest, told Brit that his half brothers weren't afraid to play dirty.

"Perhaps a bit of leverage may turn things in your favor," Jack said thoughtfully.

*Leverage...*

Brit had leverage as the legal heir, to the title and fortune, but the stipulation of marriage by his next birthday negated that leverage as a true threat. In his experience, a two-pronged approach was always best. He would need something more... The memory of a clandestine meeting in a dark corridor, lash-fringed eyes lowering as Raven Cratchit closed the distance between them, rising onto her toes, gave Brit the beginnings of an idea. One that just might work.

"Wexford House, it is," Brit said decisively.

Belinda tumbled forcibly through the wooden door, her feet flying out from under her as the feeling of floating stole her stomach. She hated flying. One might think the ability to hover in the air and move through objects would be an advantage of the nonliving but for Bel, it only served as a reminder of her undesirable predicament.

She had lived as a spirit for two years and three hundred and twelve days, and every one of those days she'd wished she could turn back time and stop herself from taking those pills. Most of the time, she didn't even think of herself as dead. That way lie madness.

"It took you long enough," Archie Fox said huskily as he gathered her against his solid chest.

It was true that the moment they'd met on New Bond Street, she had been preoccupied with the rakish ghost. But his touch surprised her. Bel felt every connection from his hands on her shoulders to the alignment of their legs. She could touch the living all she liked, and it felt like little more than a soft breeze. For a few blissful seconds, Bel melted into the wondrous heat of Archie's embrace and inhaled deep the citrusy scent of his skin.

Gathering her strength, Bel leaned back to find Archie's fierce gaze locked on hers. He swooped down to kiss her, and at first, she froze. But as his warm lips slid tantalizingly across hers, Bel wound her arms around Archie's neck and clung to him as if the world was on fire and his kiss was the only thing that could save her. His head slanted as he deepened the kiss, and Bel gave in to the delicious sensations that she had never hoped to feel again. Tingles ignited in her blood, and she drove her fingers into his hair, her toes curling in her slippers.

*Lord, this man knows how to kiss.*

The thought ultimately brought her back to her senses. Such passion was the very thing that had destroyed her life.

Bel disentangled her limbs from Archie's and snapped with all of the righteous anger she could muster, "I'm not here for *that*!"

Archie lifted dark brows into the fringe of his fire-red hair and crossed his arms in front of his chest. "Then what *are* you here for?"

Bel straightened her feathered hat, swiped a hand across her wet lips, and lifted her nose. "I am here because if we do not intervene, my sister and your friend will be miserable for their entire lives. Or in Brit's case, possibly worse."

Archie stiffened, those fascinating gold-green eyes narrowing. "What do you mean by *worse*?"

Belinda glanced around her at the monkish room with its bare wood walls, a single high window, narrow bed, and side table. She had been about to request he invite her in to have a proper chat, the news she was about to impart would be best told delicately. Alas, there was nowhere to sit but the bed.

He took an impatient step toward her. "I suggest you start talking, woman."

"Woman?" Bel reared back. "Is that how you address your betters." She regretted the words as soon as they left her mouth, but something about this man's assumptions grated hard against her nerves.

"So that's how it is." Archie frowned, his eyes conveying disappointment but not surprise. "How may I assist you then, *Miss Cratchit*?" he asked stiltedly.

Humiliation, at her conceit, burned Bel's cheeks. She had grown up with next to nothing and later in life had fallen into the trap of vanity and prestige, thus her failed engagement to Lord Elliot Eaton. With hindsight, she could see Elliot had never been the right match for her—their love flared hot and then burned out in an instant.

Bel turned toward a painting that hung on the wall and studied the amateur watercolor; bright strokes depicting a sunrise reflected in a body of water. She leaned closer to read the signature. Chip Lightheart; Raven's asthmatic patient with a doggedly bright outlook. She smiled, and without turning around said, "I apologize, Mr. Fox, my manners are a bit rusty."

"I'm accustomed to wellborn lady's disdain," he replied in a flippant tone.

"That's just it." Bel faced him. "I'm not wellborn. I grew up in poverty until my father's fate changed, his money and newfound status lifting us into society. I should know better."

He bit into his bottom lip, seeming to consider whether or not to forgive her. After several agonizing moments, he gave a nod of his head and slanted her a grin. "Out with it then. What has you so worried about my mate, Brit?"

Ignoring the flutter Archie's grin evoked in her chest, Belinda swallowed and asked, "You know Brit has been arrested, yes?"

His nostrils flared as a muscle jumped in his lean jaw. "Yes, I'm aware."

"Well, I overheard John and George Griffin talking last evening." Bel took a deep, fortifying breath. If Brit's arrest made Archie angry, what she was about to tell him would likely send him into a rage. "They don't plan to stop there. John said he has no intention of losing his title, and although he didn't state a specific threat, his determination was clear as crystal. He told George they would need to stop Brit by any means necessary."

Instead of exploding with outrage, an eerie calm came over Archie, his lively face stripped of emotion, his only tell the tap of a single finger against his thigh. "The man has proven he has no ethics when it comes to getting what he wants, so your concern is valid. But what does this have to do with your sister? I've seen the doctor in action, and she does not strike me as a pushover."

Bel grinned at his accurate assessment. "That, she is not. But have you seen the way she and Brit look at one another? Their undeniable attraction when we met on New Bond Street?"

Archie's eyes lit from within as he took a step toward her. "I was a wee bit preoccupied with the most fascinating woman I've met in my life." His mouth quirked. "Or my death."

Bel could flirt with the best of them, but she resisted her natural inclinations and the indisputable draw she felt toward the man before her. "Raven is the key to saving Brit and vice versa."

Archie stroked the auburn stubble along his cheek. "Why can't we just tell Brit and Raven what you overheard?"

Bel rolled her eyes and perched a hand on her hip. *Men!* "Because, Archie Fox, if we want them to end up together, this is a delicate situation."

"Ahh...I see." His smile did funny things to Bel's stomach. Pleasant things.

She pursed her lips, met his amused gaze, and took several sultry steps in his direction before she stopped herself and shook her head. *Putting her feelings above everything and everyone else is what had gotten her into her current untenable situation.* She raised her chin. "Later, Mr. Fox. You and I have an eternity to explore what is between us."

His shoulders slumped as he shoved his fists into his trouser pockets. "Fine. What's the plan?"

Belinda smiled wide. "I thought you'd never ask."

Brit slammed the double doors to John Griffin's office open with a bang. He'd decided to confront the man whilst still wearing the ripped suit that stank like the filth of his incarceration.

John shot to his feet, eyes wide as he shouted, "Grant!"

Brit strode forward and smacked his palms flat upon John's desk, papers fluttering. "Your butler isn't going to help you. I've sent him to the kitchens."

"Listen to me," John sputtered. "The bracelet was found. George is on his way now to clear things up with the authorities."

Jack MacCarron had taught Brit the power of active silence to loosen the tongue, so Brit straightened with a sniff. *Blimey*, he stunk.

John kept talking. "I'm certain no one will believe you took the bauble, and least of all Miss Barnacle. The girl appeared quite taken with you during dinner. In fact, I can arrange for her to join us at the theater tonight. She's an incredible gossip and once I return the bracelet to her, she will spread it far and wide that it merely slipped off her wrist during the party."

It was an olive branch and quite an effective one. If he escorted the very woman whom he'd been arrested for stealing from, any rumors of his arrest would dissolve. Not to mention, that Raven Cratchit would surely attend with her fiancé, which...Brit shouldn't care about in the least.

"Fine, I'll attend the theater." Brit crossed his arms, aware that the posture widened his shoulders. "On one condition."

"What's that?" John appeared relieved even as he wiped his palms down his trousers.

Brit spoke softly. "If you so much as frown at me in public, imply I'm less than your beloved brother returned from the dead, or jeopardize my well-being in any way, I will boot you and George out of this house and make sure every member of the ton, whom you've so graciously introduced me to, knows what a lying bastard you are."

John's pale blue eyes widened.

"Mr. Veck has already been put on notice, he made it clear that it is within my rights to claim this house and everything in it." In point of fact, he had not. But Brit could bluff with the best of them.

"But the marriage stipulation…" John sputtered.

"Only withdraws my inheritance if it is not fulfilled by Christmas. As of now, I am the Earl of Wexford." Brit leaned in. "And you bloody well better start treating me like it."

A moment of silence stretched out, John's face turning florid in the morning light.

"Are we agreed?" Brit prompted.

"Yes." John swallowed. "I'll have a footman deliver the invitation to Miss Barnacle while you get some rest. Truly, Brit, it was all a horrid misunderstanding."

But even as the man spoke the apology, Brit could see the wheels turning behind his eyes. They were half brothers by blood after all, and Brit too had that inexplicable drive within him to never give up. It was an instinct he'd realized while living on the streets that not everyone possessed. When faced with horrific obstacles, most took the path of least resistance. Yet those same obstacles drove Brit to strive higher. If he'd decided his little gang would have ham for Christmas, he would do whatever it took to fulfill that promise. Brit set goals and never wavered from them. It was how he'd not only survived but kept so many urchins under his care alive as well. He always had contingency plans for his contingency plans.

John's calculating gaze made Brit think that perhaps his perseverance had come from their mother because John was clearly not giving up easily either.

Without another word, Brit turned on his heel and dragged his exhausted body up the stairs, realizing that the comfort of the orphanage had made him complacent. He'd let his survival instincts slip. And look where it had gotten him.

After ordering a bath, Brit entered his room and closed the door behind him. The exhaustion should have him collapsing, instead he felt like a wild cat. He paced the confined space, every step ratcheting his restless anger higher. He wanted to hammer John's soft face in; twist his arm behind his back and bring him to his knees. The man had taken advantage of Brit's trust. But even more so, Brit was angry with himself. His new *brothers* had given him laudanum and watched him choke on it, and yet, Brit had come back for more. He had trusted their words instead of their actions. Somehow, he still longed for their approval, for connection, for *family*.

How incredibly stupid he'd been.

With an explosive growl, he threw his body into a punch and slammed his fist into the wall. Wood and skin splintered on impact, the pain popping the bubble of his rage.

Brit bent at the waist and sucked in air as if he'd run for hours. All the years while teaching at Hill Orphanage, he'd thought he'd left behind the pain of his past, vanquished the pent-up anger inside. But he'd simply outrun it for a while. Fury still simmered like poison in his soul.

Brit straightened and pushed out a breath as a dastardly plan took shape in his mind. His fight with John Griffin wasn't over. Not by a long shot. The man would pay dearly for his transgressions, and Brit would keep the earldom in the process.

Raven was the key to it all.

# Chapter Twelve

*The boy, raised to believe Christmas a hallowed event, bolstered up his courage and said, "Christmas a humbug, sir? You don't mean that, I am sure."*

*"I do," said Scrooge. "What right have you to be merry? You're poor enough."*

*The snow began falling in fat flakes, bathing the boy's nose and lashes, those same flakes melting on Scrooge's ruddy nose, his mouth pressed in an unyielding line, blocked the boy's entrance into the house.*

As the lights went down and the curtain opened, Raven couldn't breathe. With Jonathan on her right and Brit on her left she sat rigid, afraid to move a muscle lest she reveal the source of her discomfort. Utterly aware of every shift of Brit's legs and the movements of his strong, fine hands, his presence beside her was like a living fire that could scald if she got too close. His knee brushed her skirt and she nearly leapt out of her skin.

Breath shallow, Raven did not dare shift away from him for fear that John may sense something amiss. She thought of linking her arm through John's or taking his gloved hand in hers to cover a move away from his brother, but, alas, her fiancé was not one for public displays of affection, even in a pitch-dark theater.

So, she sat motionless; back straight, knees locked, hands clenched in her lap watching the drama of *Othello* play out far below her on the stage. She'd seen the production countless times, this version appeared different however when Othello himself appeared on the stage as a man dressed as a woman tripping onto her face, his riotous wig of blonde curls flying across the floor. The audience burst out laughing. And in that moment, the dark figure on her left moved.

"Tis rather hot in here." The deep whisper came so close to her ear that a shock tingled down her spine. As luck would have it, another chuckle rippled through the crowd and a furtive glance at John confirmed he hadn't noticed the tension between her and his brother. The December night had turned warm, causing the theater to feel stifling. But Raven straightened, determined to ignore Brit's comment.

A moment later, she felt the slide of her heavy bracelet as it turned against the silk of her glove. With a furtive glance down, she could make out one of Brit's long fingers turning it on her wrist as if to inspect the jewels for their veracity. He leaned into her again, and she had to strain to make out the low tones of his voice.

"I wonder at my brother trusting something so..." He paused, and his breath tickled the hairs by her ear, goosebumps tingling down her neck. "...*exquisite* this close to me in the dark."

Suppressing a shiver, Raven focused on the intent behind his words and detected a hint of humor. Or was it irony? He placed his index finger on a large ruby and gave it a light press, then pulled back his gloved hand. The bracelet had arrived at the house as she'd readied for the theater, another extravagant gift from John, precipitating a change into a new scarlet silk gown with a bustled skirt and an off-the-shoulder neckline.

The press of wool gaberdine against that exposed shoulder sent her pulse throbbing into the tips of her fingers.

"You look lovely, Raven," Brit whispered.

Heat flew up her neck and into her cheeks. What was the cad thinking? Firstly, he must know that she could not risk talking to him, lest she alert the man beside her. Secondly, Brit had escorted Clemintine Barnacle to the theater and the girl sat on his opposite side, shooting him doe-eyed gazes of longing every chance she got.

Did Brit hope to annoy John with his inappropriate attention? Raven sensed some new hostility between the brothers, for obvious reasons.

Raven had not wanted to believe Brit a jewel thief, in fact, could not understand what would motivate him to steal, but the memory of his slipping the necklace from her throat the very night Clemintine's bracelet went missing, had given her pause. Had he not admitted to her that he'd stolen to survive? Perhaps it had become an impulse that he could not resist even though he no longer needed the money.

Her right hand fluttered up to her throat, realizing belatedly that she had left her engagement locket on her vanity table at home.

Brit moved closer, the hard muscle beneath his coat pressing into her shoulder as he whispered, "Forget something?"

She tilted her head from side to side so that to anyone else—who wasn't pressed up against her in the dark theater—it would appear she stretched her neck. But as she turned toward Brit, she hissed, "That is none of your concern."

Thankfully, Clemintine tugged on Brit's other sleeve drawing his attention as she chattered for the remainder of the first act. The play droned on, the audience's hilarity buzzing like a horde of flies through Raven's dazed mind. She could not focus on the dialogue or the visual spectacle playing out before her as Brit slouched in his seat, widening the spread of his long legs, his knee pressing against her leg.

Raven's temperature rose several degrees.

She thought to move away, a slight shift of her position would disconnect the kiss of heat she could feel through the layers of fabric between them. Yet, she felt locked in place as if some invisible tether entwined them. Her skin flushed, throat tightening in exquisite torture as Brit aligned the length of his arm with hers. Whatever force kept her from moving away, also made her long to press against him and absorb more of his electrifying touch.

But she didn't dare.

When the curtains closed for intermission, Raven jumped to her feet before the announcer finished inviting the audience to partake of complimentary wassail punch and iced gingerbread biscuits in the lobby.

John stood beside her. "Are you quite all right, my dear?"

Raven unfurled the fan that she'd forgotten hung from her right wrist and waved her face. "'Tis uncomfortably warm in here, is it not?"

"Let us get you some punch." He took her elbow and steered her toward the back of the box.

"A most excellent idea, *brother*!" Brit heralded as he moved to Raven's other side.

Raven's gaze pivoted to Brit. Did she imagine the mocking tone he used? When he smiled down at her beatifically, she swiveled back to John whose pinched expression made his annoyance clear.

"Yes, a cup of punch sounds refreshing, Lord Wexford," Clemintine gushed as she rushed up to flank Brit's other side.

Raven felt John start at the title, then deflate as he realized Clemintine addressed Brit.

They had reached the exit door and John inclined his head, gesturing for Brit to proceed them. "After you, *brother*." John made no attempt to disguise the venom in his voice.

They merged into the crowded lobby, and Raven's breathing had not regulated. She excused herself, faces blurring before her as she pushed through the merry throng, rushing into a deserted corridor, past the bustling ladies room and around a corner to an open window where she leaned out, gulping the cool night air.

What was wrong with her? This sort of undisciplined sentiment was unfamiliar and terribly disconcerting. She was a doctor for heaven's sake, not some naive debutant who shivered at the touch of a man!

She inhaled the fresh, winter wind, and pushed out her tangle of emotions. Brit was clearly using her to annoy his brother. Or was he? Why did she jump to that excuse instead of the obvious explanation that he was as attracted to her as she was to him? Her breath shuddered. An ineffectual situation to be sure.

"I've heard of a pulse point that can open the airways," a soft voice said behind her.

Raven didn't turn around, her heart fluttering and vision blurring as her awareness narrowed to the heat of Brit's body. His suggestion wasn't far off, and she suddenly wished she'd brought her kit of acupuncture needles.

"Or a bit of punch." He moved to her side and held out a small cup.

Raven grasped the mug, lifted it to her mouth, and drained it in one drink. Refreshment mingled with the burn of alcohol in her throat as relief smoothed her ragged nerves, and she let out a slow exhale.

"Better?" Brit asked, his mouth tilting in a closed-lip smile.

Instead of answering, she focused on his stupidly attractive face and spat, "What game are you playing?"

He leaned a shoulder against the wall. "I don't see this as a game."

"Then what *do* you see it as? Because I don't appreciate being toyed with."

His lips compressed, his dark gaze capturing hers. "Did you know I spent last night in jail?"

Raven felt her mouth drop open.

"And before you ask, I didn't take the bracelet."

"Then why..." Her question split into too many branches to voice. *Why were you arrested? Did the Barnacles press charges? Why does Clemintine not care? Why did you take my necklace off my throat? Did you really grow up on the streets as a thief?*

He raked a hand through the waves of his hair. "John had me arrested, and I suspect he took the bracelet himself since it conveniently turned up the next morning."

"He wouldn't do that." Raven's first inclination was to defend her fiancé.

"Wouldn't he?" Brit arched an ebony brow.

Raven stilled. John had shown sides of himself since his brother's return that she had not previously witnessed. Possessiveness. Disregard for her profession. Barely suppressed anger and impatience. But was it more than that? Did the man she hoped to marry possess such vindictiveness as to throw his own brother in jail? She could not believe it. "I think you're inventing battles that aren't there," she finally said, unsure if she said it for Brit or herself.

"You don't believe your precious fiancé might do something to discredit me so that he doesn't lose his fortune and precious title?" he challenged.

"I..." The churn of Raven's gut was answer enough.

"Thus, my need for your help," he said lifting his square chin.

Raven studied Brit's face. Something was different about him. A hardened set to his jaw, a slight frown tugged down his lips, and his eyes, those wild, dark pools, sparked with a fire she didn't recognize from the kind man she thought she knew. "The proposition, you mentioned before," she said almost without meaning to.

"Precisely. I find that I am swimming in a dark ocean full of creatures that I've never encountered. I need a guide; someone who can shine a light and advise me on how to navigate my unfamiliar environment." Brit winced at his reproachful analogy of the society to which she belonged. "I mean—"

Raven raised her brows dubiously. "I know precisely what you mean. But why me? I'm barely tolerated in polite society myself. I did not grow up in it, and my profession keeps me well on the fringes of most ladies' acquaintance."

Gaze narrowed; he rubbed a thumb across his jaw in contemplation. "I'd like to know more about your past when we have the leisure to discuss it, but you've just confirmed precisely why I need your assistance."

"I'm afraid I do not follow."

He leaned toward her slightly. "I don't have hopes, nor do I aspire to be at the center of London's ton. I merely wish to fit in enough so that I may find a wife."

"Oh?" To Raven's mortification, the word came out as a squeak.

Brit gave a casual shrug. "As part of my entailment, I must acquire a suitable wife before my next birthday or forfeit my inheritance."

"Then you need look no further than the lady you arrived with tonight," Raven replied in a clipped tone that had nothing to do with the heat in her chest as she envisioned Clemintine Barnacle, one of the most annoyingly condescending women of her acquaintance, married to the barely civilized man before her. The match was preposterous.

Without warning, Brit stepped forward and took her gloved fingers in his. "I said, suitable," he whispered as his thumb made a circular motion across the back of her hand. Raven couldn't speak, and yet, felt herself step closer to him as she looked up into the face that haunted her day and night. Was he implying...?

The chime of bells signaled the end of intermission neared, and they jerked apart, but Brit held tight to her hand. "Will you help me?"

Raven clenched her teeth and her wits returned. "What do I get out of this?"

He cocked his head. "Get out of what?"

"You said you had a proposition for me which implies there is an exchange of favors." Raven tugged her fingers from his and ignored the regret she felt at the absence of his large, warm hand cradling hers, then she lifted her chin. This was a chemical attraction. Biology. Nothing more.

His full mouth lifted on one side, pulling out a long dimple. "Time with me, of course."

Raven reeled back at the sheer audacity of the man. Her response left her lips before she gave it too much thought. "No."

Brit took her arm as she turned away, but she shrugged him off. "We need to get back before we are missed. Miss Barnacle is the answer to all your problems, Lord Wexford. And she has likely already sent out the cavalry to find you, so I suggest you return posthaste," Raven muttered the last as she walked swiftly around the corner, putting distance between them, and although she could feel him behind her, he was wise enough not to push her further.

A wave of shame washed over her. How had she allowed herself to be diverted by a pretty face and a wide set of shoulders? She was no worse than Clementine falling at the handsome lord's feet!

Just before she reached the lobby, she shot the exasperating man a warning glare over her shoulder and he stopped, allowing her to proceed him. Raven flew straight to John who awaited her by the door leading to their box. His countenance appeared stormy until she linked her arm through his and gazed up into his eyes. "My apologies, the heat is causing me to feel a bit ill."

Whatever he read in her face must have convinced him because his frown melted, and he patted her hand. "We will go, my dear. I'll have the carriage brought around."

As they moved toward the exit, Raven couldn't stop herself from looking back at the dark figure lurking in the shadows. The intensity of Brit's gaze told her this wasn't over.

Brit tugged off his cravat with a bit too much haste, the fabric tightening against his throat, strangling. In his experience, a solid threat backed up by action threw the enemy off balance. Distract and disarm. Preferably with an action your opponent did not expect. It was a simple plan really; steal Raven from John, devastating his opponent emotionally and socially whilst allowing Brit to gain his inheritance all in one blow.

But his leverage refused to cooperate. If he wished to win Raven Cratchit over, they would need an excuse to spend time together outside of his brother's watchful gaze. A reason that Brit had constructed and presented to her at the theater. He had read on her face that she wanted to, and yet, she had refused.

He could see how his presence and especially his touch disconcerted her. The normally composed doctor blushed and became fidgety, her words flustered, voice breathless. He yanked off the cravat and tossed it onto the washstand. The problem lay in the way *she* affected *him*. When he gazed into those lavender-blue eyes, he fell backwards in time, to a place before...*Before what?*

His head aching, Brit sank down on the bed and squeezed his eyes tight, the memory of Raven facing off with him in the corridor as vivid as a picture—candle flames burnishing the rounded curve of her cheeks and darkening her lush lips, delicate jaw set, body tense against the onslaught of his flirtation. His gut tightened at the memory of her stepping closer to him, seemingly against her will.

He could not deny that Raven Cratchit stirred something within him that he thought long lost; a boldness, a feeling of being more present in the moment, more *alive*.

When was the last time he'd felt that mischievous delight? That joyous anticipation?

Brit's eyes popped open.

Being with her felt like winning a huge score and taking it back to the Saffron Hill hideout; Archie, Chip, and the others whooping with joy over the fresh bread and sausages or sack of coins or whatever loot that Brit had procured.

When had he last felt that alive and happy? Teaching at the orphanage gave him a certain sense of satisfaction and security; he no longer had to fight for his next meal or wonder if the fire might burn out during the night leaving his nose bitten with frost, his fingers frozen stiff. But he could admit something was missing from his life...or had been.

Brit shot to his feet and began to pace.

The moment he'd stared into Raven's I-will-not-allow-you-to-die-today gaze, something had ignited inside of him; a flame that only she could kindle. A fire Brit did not want to live without. He needed her passion, her kindness, her light to extinguish the darkness inside of him.

He stopped at the frosted window and stared at vaulted rooftops and belching chimneys that stretched toward a luminous moon, and longing ached in his chest. It wasn't about the inheritance or even stealing the title from John. Brit didn't know if he could survive losing someone as vibrant and passionate and perfect for him as Raven Cratchit.

For years, he had thought he'd wanted peace and safety. He'd chastised himself for feeling restless at the orphanage and convinced himself that he was content. Even as his soul longed for more than just to survive. He needed the excitement of the unknown to thrive. He needed a woman by his side who would push him to become more, to give him a focus and a purpose. He hadn't thought he'd wanted the money or the title. But all he'd needed was a reason to claim it. Between the resources and influence of the earldom, and Raven's doctoring skills and unrelenting drive, they could change the world. Together.

Suddenly, winning Raven's heart was no longer a means to an end, a way to anger his brothers and gain vengeance, but the only end he would accept. His heart hammered against the cage of his ribs and Brit recognized the fear coursing through his veins. Admitting what he wanted meant he now had a lot to lose, and part of him wanted to run as far away from Raven Cratchit and his entitlement as possible.

Perhaps this was a very bad idea.

His gaze shifted to the painting of Santorini and its pristine white buildings with vivid, blue-tiled roofs. A world away from the smog and clouds of London. Perhaps, there were teaching jobs in

Greece where he could track down his mother's relatives and live a peaceful life by the sea. No risk. No potential to have his beating heart ripped from his chest.

He fisted his hands until his nails dug into the flesh of his palms.

At Holy Trinity, where he attended church with everyone at Hill Orphanage, he'd recently heard a scripture that had stuck with him: *God hath not give us a spirit of fear, but of power, and of love, and of a sound mind.*

*Power and love and a sound mind...*

Brit would need all three of those virtues in order to fight the fear urging him to run from heartache and win the woman he had never dared dream could exist, let alone be his.

Archie blended seamlessly into the shadows. The one advantage to being dead was his ability to hide in plain sight. If he'd been able to pull that off as a youth, he would've been the best bloomin' tooler the world had ever seen.

Nor would he have ended up hiding from the pain of his past in an opium haze or been killed by a dealer he could no longer pay. *The barrel of a gun loomed in his face; his cocky assurances that he could get the money when his pockets were empty and he'd already stolen from everyone he cared for. The bludger's calm voice as he said it was too late, an example had to be made. The terrible knowledge that he'd miscalculated; run out of time. BOOM!*

Archie's vision went black as his heart galloped like a runaway horse.

"Deep breaths, Arch." He inhaled shakily and then blew out the panic seeping into his veins. Brit had found him in the alleyway. Archie had watched his big, strong friend bow over his empty body and break down in racking sobs. Brit had blamed himself.

It was long over, and nothing could be done about all the hurt he'd caused. But he *could* save his best friend. If he could stay out of his head and anchored to the moment.

The old codger that frequented the grounds of Hill House had told Archie time and again that accepting forgiveness and forgiving oneself was the only way forward. But Archie wasn't ready for the light. Not yet.

His gaze darted to the spirit shimmering like diamonds in the sun. Belinda Cratchit lifted her finger to her lips and pointed down toward the staircase.

A floorboard creaked, the furtive sound of someone creeping through the night.

Brit had retired hours ago and after his night of incarceration, slept like the dead. So, when Belinda had overheard John's new plan to defame Brit, they had decided to handle it themselves. But in order to impact the living, he would need to ground himself in reality.

Archie bounced on the balls of his feet, and raised his arms, touching the walls on either side of the doorway. He felt the cool wood and grooves of the paneling as he puffed air in and out of his lungs. This was for Brit. He would not let his best mate down again.

As his eyes popped open, he spotted the maid, Ines, wearing a thin wrapper, golden hair flowing down her back as she tiptoed along the corridor, holding a single candle. Her eyes were wide and searching, her mouth set in a determined line.

The Griffin brothers' plan was diabolical, yet simple. They had paid the young chambermaid enough to buy back her sister's debt to a workhouse. The Griffins had even arranged for the girl's promotion to upstairs maid in a lesser household on the edge of the city so she could continue to support her sibling. All Ines had to do was slip into Brit's chamber while he slept, place some of her torn clothing around the room, and allow herself to be found naked in his bed in the morning.

To ensure validity of the claim, Bert the valet would be the one to find them and would call for John, who would be waiting close by and come running to confirm that Brit had physically accosted the poor maid.

Charges would be brought and although they would most likely be dismissed given Brit's noble title, the scandal would be enough to discredit Brit in all of polite society and ensure he did not find a suitable wife in the week leading up to Christmas and his birthday.

Bel hissed Archie's name, drawing him out of his contemplation, and he sprang into action, jumping forward and blowing out the candle in the maid's hand.

Ines yelped and froze to the spot.

Belinda, who had maintained a more solid physical hold on the world—perhaps because her death had occurred more recently than Archie's—stomped down the hallway toward the girl, her footsteps pounding and quick.

Ines spun around to face the sound and cried, "Who's there?"

When no one answered, the maid turned back and doggedly crept forward.

During their time together, Archie and Bel had discovered that if they touched, their spirit forms became temporarily more solid. When they'd kissed for the first time—*what a kiss*—they had been in the Cratchit's back hallway and nearly scared the wits out of a footman who caught a glimpse of them in the shadows before they disappeared again.

Visibly trembling, Ines had almost reached Brit's door when Archie and Bel raced ahead of her, linked hands, and shimmered into view.

The girl shrieked and stumbled on the hem of her wrapper, falling onto her backside.

"Leeaveee this hoouussse...and do nooot retuuuurn," Bel moaned as they hovered over Ines's shaking form.

"Or join us in the hereafter," Archie boomed.

Ines crab-walked backward from their looming forms, her mouth opening and closing, eyes wide as saucers.

Archie and Bel floated off the ground and waved their arms as they said in unison, "Go or die!"

The maid scrambled to her feet and ran, stumbling down several steps before regaining her balance and tearing out the front door.

Laughter burst from Archie's chest, and he released Bel's hand so as not to traumatize everyone in the house. He couldn't remember the last time he'd laughed with pure joy.

"I hope she doesn't freeze out there," Bel said, her adorable nose scrunched in concern.

"She'll be fine. Her beau in the stables will keep her warm enough," Archie quipped.

Bel spun towards him. "What if she comes back and tries again?"

Archie took Belinda's hand and led her into an empty room where he tugged her gently into his arms. He didn't think he'd ever felt anything better than the perfect fit of her body against his; she was comfort and passion, and her scent was like roses in sunshine. He tucked his nose into her hair and breathed deep, then said, "I'll stay here and watch over him. The Shadow said minimal involvement, but if she returns, I can at least wake Brit before the plot can play out."

"What about the next time John attempts something?" Bel said, her words hot and tantalizing against the skin of his neck. Good heavens, he could spend forever right there in her arms.

He sighed with contentment, his voice low as he said, "All we have to do is get him through the week, and if all goes to plan, by Christmas our job will be done."

# Chapter Thirteen

*Something rose within the boy, something that lay dormant but always awoke when he needed it most. He squared his small shoulders and the words flowed from him without his seeming volition. "What right have you to disparage this sacred night, Mr. Scrooge? You are rich enough!"*

*With a glower, Scrooge returned, "And yet that gold does not fill my belly, does it now?"*

*And with that pronouncement, the old man stepped back into the warmth of the house and slammed the door shut in the boy's face.*

It took two days for Brit to work up his courage. So, when he stopped on the Cratchit's doorstep, he started to engage the knocker, then lowered his hand again. He knew little of making formal calls and less of courtship rules, especially when the lady was already spoken for. What the bloomin' hell was he thinking to show up at her home without an invitation?

Another, darker voice whispered, *And a street kid in a monkey suit, at that.*

Brit turned around, skipped down the three stairs to the walk, then stopped, pivoted, and stared up at the cheery blue door. *God did not give you a spirit of fear...* "Nor have I ever been a bloody coward," he muttered and climbed back up the steps, envisioning the glow in Raven's eyes when she looked at him. He had not imagined their connection. This woman was worth the potential for humiliation.

With a nod, he banged the knocker three times, then straightened his coat, and lifted his chin, rehearsing his introduction and reason for visiting. As he heard footfalls approaching, it occurred to him belatedly that he should have a card of some sort. He patted his pockets as if one might magically appear.

A man who must have been a hundred years old, opened the door with a gap-toothed smile and asked in a cockney accent, "May I help ye, young sir?"

Responding to the informality and friendliness of the servant, Brit smiled. "I'm Brit Griffin, here to call upon Miss Cratchit."

The man's smile widened, pale eyes blinking rapidly. "My days! If it ain't the new Lord Wexford. Come in, come in! I'm Trotty, the butler. Tis a high pleasure ta meet ye, m'lord."

Brit should have anticipated that he would not need a calling card when his return from the "dead" had been front page news in all the London papers from the society sheets to *The Times*. The sketches of him ranged from caricatures that exaggerated his jawline and inflated the width of his shoulders, to the eerily accurate portraits that allowed people on the street to bow or call out his name. Quite disconcerting if he was honest.

With a nod to Trotty, Brit entered the warmth of the foyer and thought for a moment that he'd stepped into a forest, so strong was the scent of pine. Evergreen branches draped over every eve and doorway, each swag dotted with crimson bows, and tied with candied orange slices. He turned and nearly jumped as he came face to face with a pair of life-sized nutcrackers, standing sentinel on either side of the main corridor; one in the royal guardsmen attire of a black, bearskin cap, signature red coat, and gold buttons, while the other wore a red and green plaid kilt, a fuzzy tam, and held realistic-looking bagpipes.

Peals of laughter echoed down the hall as the butler took Brit's top hat, and said, "Ye've come at a most opportune time, m'lord."

"Why's that?" Brit asked, handing over his greatcoat.

The little man's eyes sparkled. "Tis the Cratchit's Christmas Spectacular."

Brit arched his brows as he spotted a skirted figure dart across the end of the corridor. "I need two more minutes!" she laughed.

Had that been Raven? She looked like a young girl with her dark hair streaming behind her, a red bow waving like a streamer among the strands.

"This way, if ye please." The butler motioned for Brit to follow him into the house. A snippet of *Up on the Housetop* was sung off-key followed by a masculine chortle, the same voice beginning a countdown from five. "Four...three..."

"I cannot reach to place..."— there was a delicate grunt— "my star!"

Brit turned toward the sound of the familiar voice calling out in distress to find a small library, the shelves stuffed to overflowing, the floor and tables and even the chairs cluttered with haphazard piles of books. Raven balanced on one foot, straining to place a pearl-covered star on the pinnacle of a pine.

"...two..." the voice boomed from the other room.

Brit, quickly assessing that this was some sort of competition, rushed into the room, plucked the star from Raven's hand, and placed it over the top spindle just as the man finished his countdown and shouted, "Time's up! Step back from your trees, Cratchits!"

Raven gave a start and whirled to face him, a rebuke dying on her lips as their eyes met. "Brit!"

He offered a crooked grin. "The one and only."

"What are you...I mean..." Raven trailed off, her cheeks flags of pink, careless waves falling around her face from her partially pulled back hair, her glorious lavender eyes never leaving his face. The always-in-control doctor blinked up at him as if he were some sort of wonderous apparition—her gaze splendidly unguarded.

Brit's heart pounded too fast, the space between them charged like the air after a lightning strike. His gaze roved down her face to her full, parted lips, slender throat, and her chest heaving as if she could not catch her breath. His limbs felt suddenly heavy, his thoughts dull.

"Raven, you better not be cheating," a voice said from the doorway.

Raven turned first. "Of course not, Tim. How dare you imply such treason!" Her words were softened with a grin.

Brit raked the hair off his forehead and turned to find a young man in his early teens with enormous brown eyes, a slim build, and an elfin face.

Tim's gaze narrowed on Brit. "Not even with your staarrr?" he drew out the last word tauntingly.

Raven's shoulders slumped.

"Ha! Caught you!" Tim did a quick dance as he pointed at Raven.

"I did very little," Brit explained. "The tree was already glorious without the star."

"No worries, mate," Tim said with a grin. "Raven has won the last three years in a row. Someone had to topple her crown." The boy patted Raven's shoulder, his smile widening.

Raven gave the back of his arm a hard pinch, making Tim yelp. "'Tis hardly my fault that I'm not tall enough to reach the top of the tree."

He rubbed his arm and turned to Brit. "To whom do I owe my debt of gratitude?"

Brit extended his hand. "Brit Griffin."

"The new earl!" The boy declared with a comical expression. "Did you really grow up in the Amazon rainforest with the pygmies? I can't quite imagine it, given your height."

Laughter exploded from Brit's chest. Unable to speak, he shook his head before he finally said, "No, but that might be the most imaginative theory I've heard."

Tim finally shook Brit's hand. "Tim Cratchit, the youngest and most likable."

"I don't doubt it," Brit replied.

"I would protest," Raven said as she ruffled the boy's already disheveled hair. "But he's quite right."

Tim chuckled and then sprinted out of the room, calling, "Ma, Raven disqualified herself!"

Mrs. Cratchit appeared in the doorway. "Oh, hello there, Mr...er...my lord." The woman dipped into a hurried curtsy.

"I prefer Brit if you please." Brit took Mrs. Cratchit's hand, pulling her up. "I haven't quite adjusted to the title."

"I can understand why." She smiled warmly. "Since you are here, we could use your help. Normally the servants judge our contest, but they are hardly impartial."

Brit glanced at Raven in question, and she gave an uncharacteristic shy nod of assent.

He could see that he'd unbalanced her with his appearance at such a familial occasion. Good. Perhaps the setting combined with his determination to be candid would give them the opportunity for a fresh start.

They entered a large morning room where a Christmas tree stood in a place of purpose, towering two stories high, covered in glittering beads and glass ornaments of gold and silver. Raven's older sister Martha sat cross-legged by the murmuring fire, poking cloves into plump oranges wrapped in festive ribbon. While Peter and Matthew—the middle brother—strung fluffy, white popcorn and crimson berries into a garland. Brit had met Peter at the orphanage but barely recognized the stoic doctor as he laughingly threw cranberries at Matthew's head. Tim channeled his exuberance into playing an up-tempo version of "Hark the Herald Angels Sing" on a stately baby grand piano.

The scene was altogether wholesome. Brit swallowed an inexplicable lump in his throat. What would it have been like to grow up in an environment of such love and acceptance? He glanced over at Raven, perhaps her family's love fostered the confidence and sense of purpose that had birthed the extraordinary woman's dream to become London's first practicing female physician.

"Attention everyone!" Mrs. Cratchit clapped her hands, drawing the activity to a halt. "We have a guest judge for our spectacular this year. The Earl of Wexford, Brit Griffin."

Brit smiled and twirled his hand as he bent in an exaggerated bow.

The Cratchits dropped their trimmings, including Bob Cratchit who appeared from behind the massive pine and stood before him. Martha curtsied low while the men bowed deep.

"There is no need to stand on such formalities, unless…" Brit quirked a brow. "You hope to win my favor."

His joke hit the mark and the Cratchits relaxed.

Matthew, who appeared in his twenties, with light brown hair and an oddly familiar countenance, stepped forward and said with mock affront, "Tis hardly fair when Raven saved your life, is it?"

"No worries, old man." Tim clapped his older brother on the shoulder. "She has right disqualified herself by accepting Lord Wexford's help."

"You don't say." Matthew's eyes narrowed in calculation as the other Cratchits all spoke at once.

Peter cupped his jaw shrewdly. "Can I offer you a brandy or a cigar, my good man?"

Matthew moved in front of Peter. "You look like a discerning gentleman. How about a piece of Cook Fran's famous mince pie?"

"You are all despicable!" Raven laughed and turned to Brit. "This man is above reproach. Now show him your trees and let's be done with this."

"The reigning champion is a sore loser, it would seem," Martha muttered.

"You bet your gumdrop buttons, I am! I planned that theme for months." Raven's lips pursed in an adorable pout.

Raven's tree had silk butterflies perched on nearly every branch, their wings lustrous shades of lavender, pink, and silver. The matching glass baubles caught the sunlight, while glittering, metallic ribbons flowed down the sides, curling up at the ends. It had been the most colorful, creative concoction Brit had ever seen.

Until he saw the other Cratchits' trees.

Each family member had space in a different room to decorate their own tree, all of them glorious and unique. Mrs. Cratchit's tree in the sewing room was sheathed inside a flowing, white gown with gold trim that she had stitched by hand. Wings with real feathers extended out on either side to give the illusion of an angel. Mr. Cratchit's tree, in the front parlor, was festooned with different-sized green and silver drums, wooden music notes, and pieces of sheet music. Matthew's had a train theme, and Martha's held dozens of gingerbread houses and tiny people decorated with frosting and colorful candies.

Peter had forgone the pine altogether and stacked books in the shape of a tree that nearly hit the ceiling. The engineering of the near-perfect symmetry was impressive, if not entirely festive.

But it was Tim's tree that had all of them grinning from ear to ear. Tiny legs covered in striped tights with pointed slippers protruded from the tree at random angles, as if elves dove inside the branches. Comical little faces peeked out among swirling peppermints and oversized candy canes. But perhaps the best part was that the tree was topped with an enormous, candy-striped stocking cap, and a pair of curl-toed shoes tipped with bells jutted out of the bottom; creating the illusion that a giant elf held the tree upright.

Overall, the tree was a jumble of red, white, and green chaos that conveyed humor and joy, just like the boy himself.

Brit stroked his chin. This was the final tree, and the decision was upon him. Mrs. Cratchit pushed a golden ornament into his hands that read, *Cratchit Christmas Champion 1864.*

"The winner's name will be engraved upon the trophy, and it shall be hung upon our main family tree with the previous years' winners," she said.

"At least this year," Matthew said with a wiggle of his brows. "It won't be Raven's name. Thanks to you, Lord Wexford."

"Please call me Brit. After this, I feel like I've earned the familiarity."

"Well then, Brit," Mr. Cratchit boomed. "We await your decision!"

Brit's gaze shifted to Raven who smiled wide as her eyes darted to Tim's playful tree. He offered her a wink, then moved to face the family. "You all have created the most marvelous Christmas displays I've ever witnessed, even more creative than the grand trees at Harrods."

There were smiles and nods all around.

"That's because we honor the true meaning of Christmas in our hearts," Martha said merrily.

"Well then, I must award the tree that brought me the most joy. Quite the most whimsical thing I've witnessed, perhaps ever." Brit extended the trophy to the youngest Cratchit whose mouth dropped open as he accepted the large bauble. "Tim Cratchit, I declare you the winner of the Cratchit Christmas Spectacular!"

Tim let out a whoop as he jumped up, and punched the air, shouting, "God bless the new Lord Wexford!"

The Cratchits laughed even as the Mr. and Mrs. smiled at their youngest indulgently.

"Well done, old chap," Peter said amiably.

"Tim, how did you do this?" his mother asked in wonder.

"Are you certain you didn't have any help?" Matthew challenged.

"If by help you mean using you as a model, then yes," Tim said and promptly ran from his brother's lunge.

"Don't you break that ornament!" Mrs. Cratchit shuffled after her two youngest as they raced out of the room.

The others followed, chattering about each other's trees. Which left only Brit and Raven in the room.

"Well done, Brit," she said, gazing up at him, her clear amethyst eyes twinkling.

They stared at one another a moment too long before Brit said in a rough whisper, "Thanks for allowing me to participate in your family tradition."

"Oh, it isn't over yet." Raven smiled at him, the expression lighting her entire countenance as her gaze roamed over his face. "There's so much more to come."

For some unknown reason, Brit's heart began to thump so loudly, he worried she might hear it. Yet, he could not look away. A connection snapped into place between them with such force that someone might be able to see the ties of their hearts binding together if they looked closely enough. The feeling was foreign; exciting and terrifying all at once, and Brit wondered if in his vulnerability he'd just given this woman the power to shatter him.

His goal to win Raven suddenly felt incredibly foolish. He leaned back and shoved his hands into his trouser pockets, bricks of protection closing him off from his own emotions. "I should be going," he said, regretting the words, yet unable to take them back.

"I thought you needed my help?" Raven asked with a challenging lift of her brow.

She was so beautiful in that moment that she stole his breath. He could no longer remember why he'd come or why he needed to leave. "I do?" his reply came out as a question.

Raven placed a delicate hand on his arm and Brit stared at it, every one of his senses narrowed down to the point of her touch.

"Yes, something about navigating the *big, bad* creatures lurking in the fathoms of society." Her eyes sparked. She was teasing him.

His lips lifted, despite himself.

"I asked you what I got out of our bargain and I'm claiming my forfeit now," she said.

"I'm afraid to ask."

She looped her arm through his elbow and began to steer him out of the room. "Martha has won the cookie decorating contest the past five years. You're going to help me steal the title since you so heartlessly snatched the tree championship from my hands."

"Another contest!" Brit exclaimed. "I hardly think this is what's meant by honoring the true meaning of Christmas."

Raven was quiet for a moment as they walked toward the noise spilling out of the dining room. "Passively consuming the holiday is not our way. Keeping Christmas is a choice, an action. It is love and light, and the spirit in which we live year-round. What better way to stay joyful than to play games with those you love?"

"I can see that, but..." Brit trailed off as Christmastimes past flashed through his mind. All those years shivering as he watched through windows at other's cheerful gatherings, alone and frozen to the bone. Then later, thieving for weeks to keep his gang warm and fed, and that year they'd nearly lost Chip because they could not afford medical treatment. He felt himself stiffen and Raven tugged him to a stop.

"What is it?"

"What about those without?" He swallowed the emotion building in his throat. "For them, this time of year isn't a game."

She searched his face and the merriment from the other room faded away.

Brit knew his comments were unfair. Raven and Peter donated their doctoring or took payment in trade for those who could not pay.

"You speak from experience," she whispered gently.

He gave a single nod, not trusting his voice.

"If you have the time, I'll show you that there is more to our games than amusement."

This was his out. He could escape the feelings rising up to strangle him by walking out the door and not looking back. A small voice told him he stood at the crossroads of their relationship; the critical juncture of the path that once taken, he could not turn back from.

If he left, the remarkable woman who stood before him, fully unguarded and inviting, would close her heart to him forever.

Fear clawed at his throat like a living beast, urging him to run; to protect himself from the strong possibility that this could end in pain like he'd never felt. Cold logic told him the street rat would lose to the man who had been raised an earl—his brother and Raven's betrothed.

What was he even thinking?

He took a step back from her, the excuse forming on his tongue.

Then, Raven grasped his hand and smiled so big and warm that his icy reason melted away.

Brit returned her smile with a broad one of his own.

What if like Christmas, love was a choice?

Brit gave her fingers a gentle squeeze. "Lead the way, Doc Cratchit."

# Chapter Fourteen

*The cellar door gave a groan as the boy squeezed his frame through the narrow crack and into the dismal light of the space only slightly less miserable than the air, cold as bones. Not to mention the dead silence. The boy had prepared for the consequence that the miserly old bloke would tire of his services and had created a nest of blankets, stashed a few stubs of candles, and a box of Christmas biscuits that had been delivered and discarded by Mr. Scrooge—just as he himself.*

Raven watched her family, all gathered around the long dining table, working with the efficiency of an assembly line as they rolled dough, cut out festive shapes, decorated the baked cookies, and packed the cooled pastries between sheets of waxed paper in massive boxes. The entire staff were part of the production, even old Trotty.

"When did all of this start?" Brit squeezed a pastry bag full of blue-tinted icing as he decorated a gingerbread octopus with the neat, steady lines of a painter.

Somehow, Raven had known he had an artist inside him, despite his size and fierceness of manner. But when he'd begun cutting dough into the shapes of crabs, whales, and sharks, Raven had been equal parts amused and impressed. His creations were an obvious reference to the creatures lurking in the depths of high society—the very ones he'd beseeched her help to navigate.

Raven's determination to resist Brit had lasted about as long as it took her to observe the shifting awe on his face as he beheld each of her family's tree designs. The way he'd embraced their admittedly unconventional traditions and fit in so seamlessly with their playful dynamic had won her over like nothing else could have. And she had decided, for once in her life, to live in the moment.

She finished adding details to a turtle shell before replying to his question. "If you mean delivering cookies to the poor, we've been doing that since before we had the money to make more than a few dozen extra."

Brit's soul-shaking gaze captured hers and she forgot to breathe as he asked, "What do you mean, before you had the money?"

With effort, Raven broke away from his stare and replied, "We haven't always been wealthy. In fact, we were quite poor for most of my childhood." She selected another cookie and began to decorate it. "Tim was extremely ill, and we could not afford proper medical care. We almost lost him."

Brit's gaze jumped to Tim who placed finished cookies into a box while belting a rousing rendition of "Ding Dong, Merrily on High". "...in heav'n the bells are ringing...Ding dong!"

"He seems healthy enough now." Brit smiled so fondly at her brother that Raven's chest warmed, her throat flooding with emotion.

She had to swallow before she replied softly, "Yes, by the grace of God, we were able to afford treatment for him just in time."

Brit glanced back to her, a wave of dark hair falling into his eyes, the boyish look reminding her that despite the hardness she often glimpsed in him, they were nearly the same age. He swiped the lock back, and asked, "How did that come about?"

"My father worked for a miserly man who paid him little, until one Christmas, the old man showed up at our door a changed soul. He brought food and toys and made my father his equal business partner, which turned all our lives around, most of all Tiny Tim's...that's what we used to call him." Raven sighed.

"Ahh," Brit replied, understanding dawning upon his face. "So that explains all the fuss about keeping Christmas in your hearts."

"That's a big part of it, yes. Our celebrations are how we honor our heavenly savior as well as the man who turned our lives around. Joy is the highest form of gratitude, don't you think?"

Brit was quiet for a moment and then said thoughtfully, "Yes, I've witnessed this at the orphanage. Children who arrive gaunt and haunted, transform with love into flourishing, joyful rascals." He smiled, his eyes glowing from within. "I suppose it's their way of showing gratitude they don't know how to express with words."

"Exactly." Cookies forgotten, everyone in the room faded into the background as Raven asked softly, "Were you one of those orphans?"

Brit held her gaze, seeming to weigh how much of his truth he could entrust to her. "I was," he finally said. "I made a home on the streets with a ragtag gang of boys. If we wanted to eat, we stole. If we wanted to stay warm in the winter, we robbed those who had more. That's how I met Chip...and Archie."

*Archie.* Why had she forgotten to mention the spirits haunting both of their lives and the anomaly that they could each see the other's deceased loved one? Raven had noticed that lately her mind had a hard time focusing on Bel unless she was present. Wondering if Brit had the same experience, she opened her mouth to pose the question when her father's voice cut through the room, "This is the last box! Finish your cookies now, and present for judging."

"We're competing as a team," Brit declared as he took her turtle and laid it on a plate beside a remarkable likeness of an orca whale. His grin turned boyish, and she noticed hints of faded freckles across his nose. She could almost picture him as a young boy, so cute that people gladly turned their money over to him. Her chest ached at the thought.

After Raven and Brit had handily won the cookie decorating contest, Brit accompanied them to deliver cookies, wool socks, warm coats, and knit hats, along with wrapped toys to workhouses, hospitals, and orphanages across the city. Raven watched Brit kneel in front of countless children, speaking words of encouragement as he handed them a brightly wrapped parcel.

One particular boy of around four, clutched his new stuffed bear to his chest as tears tracked through the filth on his cheeks. His matted hair was surely infested with lice, yet Brit, stooped to his level, draped a coat around his narrow shoulders, and gently hugged the child close.

Raven's chest expanded and then tightened as she held back her tears at the precious sight of the strong lord, humbling himself to comfort a lost child. The image felt burned into her brain as they returned home.

Outside their townhome, the Cratchits all filed inside for a quiet family dinner. But despite her father's invitation to join them, Brit lingered outside, his hands shoved into his pockets. "Thank you for today, but I must be going," he said with an inexplicably blank expression. "I plan to speak to the MacCarrons about taking in Joey."

"Is Joey the boy from the workhouse?" Raven asked, already knowing.

"Yes. Hill Orphanage is at capacity, but I believe they'll make room for one more."

Warmth pulsed in her chest. She'd always known he was different than the gentlemen of her previous acquaintance, but he continued to prove himself a rare and honorable soul.

"Perhaps you could go after dinner?" Raven suggested hopefully.

"I would not wish to overstay my welcome."

"You heard Father. He does not extend empty invitations, unlike some of the ton." She smiled up at his handsome face and felt something inside her shift; nearly imperceptibly, yet as clear and strong as the ringing of a bell. She wanted this man in her life. Needed his smile and his laughter, his generous nature. Not for an afternoon or even as her brother-in-law. But by her side always, to talk to and live with and touch whenever she wished. She wanted this man as her own.

The change must have shown on her face because he turned fully toward her and took both her hands in his. "Raven," his voice broke on her name as his fathomless eyes searched hers. Then ever so slowly, his stare slid down to her lips.

Mouth tingling as if he'd touched it, Raven's gaze slid to his full, perfectly chiseled mouth and she stepped closer until she could feel the heat of his body, and his scent of clean pine filled her senses like a drug. His eyes darkened, his mouth set with determination and...desire. She swayed on her feet. But instead of lowering his head and taking her lips, he pulled her into his chest and wrapped his strong arms around her.

Raven sighed as her eyes fluttered closed and she nestled her cheek against the powerful curve of his chest. *Perfect.* They fit together as if they'd been born to hold one another. If she could just stay there, she would never desire another thing as long as she lived.

Snow began to fall in large, drifting flakes, melting against their heated skin.

Still, they didn't move and did not speak. The silence said it all. They...*this* was impossible.

She had promised her life to his brother and that commitment had been blessed by her father and the church, the announcement heralded throughout London. Breaking the betrothal would not only ruin her but her entire family. Not to mention destroy Brit's chances of acceptance into society as the new earl.

"I'm sorry," he whispered roughly against her hair as he released her. "I shouldn't have..." his voice trailed off and with a final searing stare, he turned and walked out of the gate.

Pain exploded in Raven's chest and tears sprung to her eyes as she watched his broad back, the tails of his greatcoat flapping behind him as he strode away, disappearing into the falling snow.

She stumbled forward to follow him, opened her mouth to shout for him to stop, to take her with him wherever he was going.

"Lucy Anne," her mother called sharply. "Come inside."

Raven stopped before she reached the gate, nails digging into clenched palms as she blinked back the tears. Slowly, she turned and made her way up the stairs and then inside where her mother waited, arms crossed in front of her plump frame. "What do you think you are doing?"

Raven glanced down the corridor, wishing she could escape. "I don't know what you mean."

"Oh, I think you do," her mother's gaze narrowed. "He is your betrothed's brother. The consequences could be—"

"Catastrophic. I know, Mother." Tears clogged her throat, her voice breaking as she said, "You needn't...worry."

Her mother's countenance softened. "Raven..." She reached out, but Raven whirled away and raced up the stairs to grieve in private.

# Chapter Fifteen

*Awaking in the midst of a prodigiously cold night, the boy felt his stomach clench in hunger. If he did not eat, there would be little purpose in hiding in Scrooge's cellar except to leave his rotting bones behind. With a bit of a tremble, he stood and made his way up the rickety stairs and into the pantry only to be assaulted by the flaring light of a candle and the shriek of the old servant woman who drove him out the side door with the stick of a broom in his back. The boy ran out through the gates, stumbling into a pile of icy slush and did not get up.*

For as long as Brit could remember, he'd had to make hard decisions. Which boy would receive the new pair of boots he'd snatched? How much food should he eat to keep up his strength without depriving the rest of the gang? Fight or run when his back was to the wall.

Not kissing Raven Cratchit in the snow had been one of the hardest.

He'd chosen flight because it was what was best for her. In that moment when he could've taken what he wanted and kissed her on the street for all and sundry to see, he'd chosen her happiness over his own. Because ruining her reputation and breaking her engagement was not the way he wanted her in his life. True, it had been his plan to steal Raven from John and marry her himself.

Which he'd failed at miserably.

But declining to follow through on his plan was the least of it, he thought as he slammed his bedroom door at Wexford House. Worse, he had gone and fallen in love with his mark. And that love would not allow him to destroy her in order to save himself.

"You look like hell, mate."

Brit spun around to find Archie lounging on his bed, arms behind his head, legs crossed at the ankles as if he belonged there.

"What are you doing here, Arch? Don't you have some lady's dressing rooms to haunt?"

Brit tossed his soggy hat onto the dresser and brushed the melting flakes out of his hair. He'd walked the twelve blocks in the snow in an attempt to cool his ardor.

"No," Archie said without humor. "But I did just spend the night with Miss Cratchit, saving you from your adoring brother's latest scheme."

Confused, Brit spun toward his oldest friend. "Miss Cratchit?"

Archie sat up and rolled his eyes. "I'm speaking of Belinda, not Raven, you lovesick dolt."

"Look who's talking," Brit retorted automatically. Then slumped into a chair by the fire to remove his boots. "What have my *brothers* done now?" He used that term in the loosest sense.

Archie stared at him for several seconds before saying, "Nothing you need to worry about because Miss Cratchit and I took care of it. It's what she overheard this morning that concerns me."

Brit arched a single brow in question.

"Bel...Miss Cratchit," he corrected himself. Was Archie Fox blushing? Brit grinned despite himself. But Archie's next words killed his humor. "She overheard John and George discuss their plans to contest the will. And if they don't succeed, who knows what they'll try next."

Brit froze with one boot dangling in his hand.

"For toffs, they're quite dastardly," Archie continued. "Your arrest proves that. I'm here to persuade you to return to Hill House."

"No." Brit had already given up enough ground that day. If he turned tail and ran from his ancestral home, he would never forgive himself.

"No?" Archie moved off the bed in a half jump, half float.

"I plan to go speak to the MacCarrons about another matter this evening, but I will not run from this Arch. I can't."

Archie stood, arms crossed, feet spread wide, assessing. Eventually, he said, "Fine. But we need a plan."

"We?" Brit's brows lifted in surprise.

"Of course, *we*." Archie looked affronted. "Who's going to watch that freakishly large back of yours, eh?"

Since Archie's death, he had seemed unable to stray from Hill House for long. When Brit had asked him about it, he'd said his soul was tied to what he'd cared about most in life. "Can you do that? I thought you were attached to the orphanage?"

"No." Archie shook his head. "I've been here every night already."

Brit blinked in confusion. "Why? I don't even want to sleep in this monstrosity of a house most of the time."

Archie's smile was slow and bittersweet. "Because I'm anchored to you, mate."

The next morning Raven arrived at the soup kitchen early. With a shiver, she wiped snow from her boots and removed her cloak, hanging it behind the door. The surly cook, Johnson, greeted her with a nod, then turned back to peeling a mountain of potatoes. The comforting scents of strong coffee, wood smoke, and bread fresh out of the oven welcomed her as Johnson pointed to a pile of freshly washed carrots and a chopping board. Raven tied an apron over her serviceable gray gown and set to work chopping.

The Cratchits were regular volunteers at St. Saviour's who cared for the  indigent, but the entire family turned out for the Christmas feast that the church sponsored with the help of donations from several congregations in the area. Her family would arrive later in the morning, all smiles and good cheer. Raven needed an escape, which the quiet kitchen and mindless work of preparing food provided.

In two short days it would be Christmas Eve and the annual Fezziwig Ball. The event did not spark the usual excitement in her chest. Perhaps because on the night of the ball, her family would announce the date of her wedding in three months' time. Her gut churned and she peeled with more vigor.

She'd awoken that morning with a melancholy she couldn't shake and done something she wasn't proud of. As she'd sat up in bed, Belinda appeared, practically glowing with excitement. Before her sister could speak, Raven had dismissed her—ordered her from her presence. It was something she'd never done since Bel had passed and was shocked to watch her sister's eyes widen as she had disappeared in a blink.

Immediately regretful, Raven had called her back over and over. To no avail.

It did not help her mood that the day before seemed to have burned so indelibly into her brain that she could not stop replaying it. Nor could she stop questioning her every word and action. And Brit's.

*Brit.*

His name felt like a prayer, a wish, a hope. An impossible dream.

Her mother was right, of course. She'd committed herself to John. But how could she live without the man who shared her ideals, sparked vibrance in her blood, and mirrored her strength of will? When Brit had held her, it felt as if two pieces of the same puzzle had been united at last. Did he feel it too?

And how cruel was it that he'd come into her life too late?

Raven slammed the cleaver down on a row of carrots, the nubs skittering across the counter and onto the floor.

"What did those vegetables ever do to you?" Matthew asked as he and Tim filed through the backdoor and brushed the snow off their coats.

Raven realized that tears welled in her eyes, and she turned away, bending to pick up the errant carrot slices.

Tim stooped beside her to help. "What is it, sister?"

"Nothing you need to worry about, Tim. Besides, you wouldn't understand," she sighed.

"I see more than people give me credit for." He insisted as they both straightened, and he began to wash the carrots in the sink. "For instance, I observed that the new Lord Wexford sees you as more than a friendly acquaintance."

Unable to help herself, Raven whirled toward her brother. "Why do you say that?"

"Because he's *always* watching you," Tim said with a sideways smirk. "He watches your reactions, your movements, and yesterday, followed you around like a puppy with his tongue lolling out of his head."

Raven crossed her arms. "I would not compare Brit Griffin to a puppy."

Tim's soulful brown eyes met hers, this boy who had endured more hardship and pain in his short life than most adults she knew, and she was forced to admit that despite his exuberance, Tim was mature beyond his years. He placed a warm hand on her shoulder. "Rave, he looks at you as if you're a miracle."

With that, Tim rushed off to chop celery.

Raven stood very still. Brit had feelings for her too. Euphoria sparkled inside her chest, and she held it close for several glorious seconds before the weight of reality snuffed her joy like a candle flame. John Griffin was her future. She had made the commitment, and she could not change her mind like some flighty socialite. Her family would pay the price.

What she felt for Brit didn't matter.

It *couldn't* matter.

The feast was in full swing, men, women, and children seated along bench seats and eating by candlelight when John appeared with a sack bursting with toys slung over one shoulder. He perched upon a small stage and began to distribute presents like an aristocratic version of Saint Nicholas, all smiles and cheer. He was a good man, Raven reminded herself. He may not light her blood on fire or look at her like she was a *blasted* miracle—Tim had to be exaggerating—but she could do far worse for a husband.

Raven handed a full plate to a homeless gentleman who accepted the food with trembling arms and tears in his eyes. "A blessed Christmas to ye, Miss."

"And you as well." She smiled, even as her heart broke. It was not enough. Cookies, a free meal here or there. Their efforts only scratched the surface of the homeless epidemic. Her gaze darted back to John, and she wondered if he'd brought the toys to placate her or if he truly cared.

Raven served another plate and another, smiling all the while. Soon, the food began to run low, and the difficult decision was made to turn away the dozens of people waiting outside. Matthew had moved to lock the doors when a broad figure ducked inside and swept off his hat, waves of midnight hair tumbling over his brow.

Brit.

Raven's heart sped as blood surged to her cheeks. What was he doing there?

Then she spotted the small person at his side—the boy, Joey, from the workhouse, but his hair was combed, skin scrubbed clean, and he wore a new set of clothes. Raven grinned, whirled around, and taking off her apron, directed Tim to take over her station.

Brit's gaze met hers across the room and locked upon her. Pulse racing, Raven made her way through the crowd. Of course, Brit had followed through with his promise to the child.

A scream cut through the air. "Help! She ain't breathin'!"

Raven stopped and searched the room, and spotting a woman on the floor, picked up her skirts to run. She pushed through the crowd that stood in a circle. "Back up if you please, I'm a doctor." She dropped down beside the gray-haired woman and began to search for a pulse. It was there but thready. The lady was unconscious and nonresponsive. Raven bent and placed her ear near the woman's mouth but could feel no exhalations. She opened the woman's coat and rose up on her knees, placing her hands over the woman's heart.

"Whot do ye think you're doin' woman?" a gruff voice demanded.

Without looking up from her patient, Raven answered. "I am about to start chest compressions because she is not breathing. I'm a physician." Peter had left for a shift at St. Bart's or she would have called for him to take over. When it came to a patient's well-being, she had no pride.

"You ain't no doctor. Stop this instant before ye kill her!" The man tugged Raven back by the shoulders.

Raven fell on her bottom. "Sir, I must insist. She needs to be revived."

"I ain't lettin' no witch touch me wife!" the man said, looming over her.

"Move away, sir." Brit appeared and held the irate man back with one large hand on the man's shoulder. "Let Doc Cratchit do her work."

"There's no such thing as a woman doctor," a younger man stepped forward to challenge Brit. "Ain't natural."

"A lady doctor is downright blasphemous, that is!" a woman squawked.

"Let go o' me this instant!" The patient's husband fought against Brit now.

Ignoring them all, Raven crawled over to the unconscious woman and began chest compressions. When that did not revive her, Raven held the unconscious woman's nose closed and blew air into her lungs.

"She's killin' 'er!"

Raven kept going, restarting her chest compressions. There was no response. She said a prayer and blew into the woman's mouth again, and again.

Finally, the patient gasped for air and began to cough.

"You're all right, ma'am," Raven assured as the woman's panicked gaze met hers. "You've had a heart incident, but—"

"Ahh!" The scream cut her off and a hard kick landed against Raven's side, sending her sprawling.

"That's enough!" Brit growled as he picked the man up and carried him bodily toward the door, ordering over his shoulder, "Martha, your sister needs help."

"I'm fine," Raven reassured, dusting off her skirt as she stood, ignoring the pain in her ribs. "We need a cab to take this woman to hospital."

Her eyes met John's over the crowd. He watched her with an unfathomable expression.

"A cab, John, if you please," Raven said stiffly.

John gave a single nod, before heading out the door.

Once the woman and her irate husband had been sent on their way with a wad of bills from Mr. Cratchit to cover her medical expenses, Raven sat in the kitchen while Martha wrapped ice in a cloth and handed it to her.

Raven took it and gingerly pressed the cold pack against her side as Martha looked on with wide eyes. "It is just a bruise, Martha. Please help Mother and the others finish the dinner."

"Are you sure this is worth it?" Martha asked with a shake of her head.

"I must ask the same question," John said, entering the kitchen. "Honestly, Raven, it really will be for the best that you put all this behind you once we are wed."

Raven's brow crinkled. "What do you mean?"

John leaned a hip against the countertop and crossed his arms, a grimace of disgust on his face. "It's not only unsafe, as you have proven today, but terribly unfeminine to touch others in such an intimate manner. You put your *mouth* on that old beggar's chapped and blistered lips. She could have infected you with God knows what! How can I allow that?"

Raven rose slowly, the pain in her ribs forgotten. "Allow?"

"Once we have a family of our own, there will be no need for you to pour all your time and energy into others," John said with a tight smile. "You will have plenty to do at home."

The kitchen door swung open, and Brit strode in, trailed by Joey who had to take three running steps to match one of Brit's. "She's off to St. Bart's," Brit announced.

"That was amazing!" Little Joey exclaimed as he ran to Raven and stared up at her with wide, unblinking eyes. "That woman wasn't alive, then she was! How'd you do that?"

Raven smiled at Joey and ruffled his hair. "With lots of practice." She looked up and met John's gaze. "And years of training."

"I want that training!" Joey shouted. "Mr. Brit, can you teach me to be a doctor too?"

"Well, that might be a challenge since I am not a doctor myself." Brit grinned down at Joey. "But once you learn to read and write, and complete your schooling at the orphanage, I'm sure any medical academy would be happy to have you."

Mr. Cratchit entered the kitchen and set an empty bowl in the sink. "Raven, Gus is bringing the carriage around to take you home. We can finish here."

"But Father, I'm fine."

"I will escort her home," John said. "My carriage is parked right out front."

Raven shot a glare at her fiancé. "That won't be necessary."

Tension filled the room for several long seconds.

Finally, Brit said, "I must return Joey to Hill Orphanage. John, why don't you come with us in *our* carriage."

Brit's words did not sound like a request.

"A solid plan," Mr. Cratchit said. "I assume we will see you at the Fezziwig Ball night after next, Brit?"

"Brit?" John lifted a brow at the informal address.

Brit smiled wide. "Yes, we go way back, don't we Mr. Cratchit."

"That we do, young man!"

Raven walked over to John. "We will finish our discussion later."

"I believe it is quite settled," John said before pivoting on his heel and stalking out of the kitchen.

Brit took a step closer to her. "Are you all right?" He raised his hand toward her and then seemed to think better of it and dropped his arm at his side.

She searched his warm, dark eyes full of concern, and perhaps a touch of the hero-worship she'd witnessed from Joey. "I…" She swallowed as emotion flooded her throat. This man would never demand she give up her doctoring career. Because he valued humans from all walks of life—rich or poor, common or genteel. And he valued her, and her wishes. Realizing they were gazing into each other's eyes, Raven swallowed and took a step back. "I am fine. Thank you, m'lord."

Strong, white teeth bit into his bottom lip as hurt played across Brit's handsome features. They had moved far past her using his title, but it was the one thing she could do to put distance between them. He gave a short bow and then called for Joey who had been eating the crumbs out of an empty pie tin, and they walked out together.

Raven slumped down on the stool, her shoulders heavy.

"What is it, darling," her father asked softly.

She shook her head and then looked up, tears shining in her eyes. "What do you do when you know you've made a terrible mistake, but to reverse it would hurt everyone you love most in the world?"

Mr. Cratchit gave her a melancholy smile. "Raven, my dear, only you can answer that question." He tucked a loose strand of hair behind her ear. "But if you are talking about what I *think* you're talking about, we Cratchits have overcome much worse."

Raven searched her beloved father's face and then threw herself into his arms. "I love you, Papa."

"And I love you, my brilliant girl." He kissed her hair and then stepped back. "I like Brit very much. We all do."

She smiled shyly. "I don't even know if he returns my feelings."

Mr. Cratchit gave a hearty laugh. "Oh, he does. Believe me, he does!"

# Chapter Sixteen

*"Whot you doin' down there, chap?" The boy barely had the inclination to raise his head, his body made of ice, all hope drained from his heart. But when he did, his gaze landed upon a rough and tumble boy near his own age with a shock of red hair and the sunny eyes of a woodland creature. "If ye provide a bit of a distraction, I'll win us some bread and tea." The boy blinked three times before accepting the outstretched hand of the newcomer who promptly tugged him to his feet and said, "Name's Archie."*

Raven's ball gown floated out in a graceful circle as she twirled before the full-length mirror. The underskirt was the softest black silk overlayed with deep purple organza and a wispy tulle sprinkled with crystals like a sky full of stars. It was quite the most magnificent gown she'd ever seen. She smoothed down the lace-trimmed, violet bodice, trying in vain to calm her trepidation. The wedding announcement loomed closer, and at least once every moment, Raven doubted she could go through with it.

"That fabric brings out your eyes."

Raven whirled to find Belinda perched upon her vanity chair.

"Bel!" Raven ran to her sister. "I'm so very sorry! I didn't mean to banish you."

"I know that, you ninny." Bel smiled. But it wasn't just any smile, this was the old Bel; her sister who could conquer the world with the curve of her lips. Joy shimmered around her like a halo.

Raven studied her. "Bel...where have you been?"

"Around, as usual," she said with a twirl of her wrist. But her eyes twinkled, and her mouth curled up at the corners.

"Around with Mr. Fox?" Raven lifted her brows.

"Mayhap." Her smile faded. "But you needn't worry about me. It's all for a good cause."

"A good cause?" Raven asked as she debated whether to wear her engagement ring. Surely it would appear suspicious if she did not. But *Brit*.

Her heart gave a squeeze. He had defended her—protected her—while she treated the unconscious woman at the shelter. While John stood back and watched, not lifting a finger until she forced his hand.

And what he'd said about not allowing her to practice medicine made her want to toss his ring into the fire to watch it tarnish and burn.

Her mother was right, of course, that the cost of breaking her engagement could have dire consequences for their family's social status. But as Father had said, they'd weathered worse and survived. Was it really worth marrying someone she was beginning to distrust? Even dislike?

She picked up the heavy emerald engagement ring. With the diamond and twilight amethyst tiara woven into her upswept hair, she hardly needed more jewelry, but she slipped the gaudy ring on her finger and turned back to her sister.

"Yes, a good cause that will be revealed in time," Bel said mysteriously.

Too preoccupied with her own drama, Raven only asked, "Will you attend the ball?"

"I wouldn't miss it for the world!" Bel declared.

The old Fezziwig Warehouse appeared like something out of a Christmas fairytale. Candelabras in a variety of colors and shapes hung from the ceiling on long chains wound in ribbons of gold and silver, their lowered height lending intimacy, as well as plentiful light, to the open space. Streamers of evergreen, dotted with crimson berries and sugar-coated plums adorned the walls and doorways. Round tables circled the room, each one topped with a unique Christmas centerpiece. There were delicate dancing ballerina dolls in sparkling tutus, swans floating in icy ponds of hardened sugar, tall glass jars full of colorful ornaments, and miniature, ceramic forests of white, pink, and gold evergreens on a bed of cottony snow. And Raven's favorite; angels with fluffy, white wings suspended on strings, flying above a humble manger.

Perhaps it was the magical environment, but an unaccountable hopefulness flickered in Raven's chest as if anything could be possible on this eve of the great miracle.

The band struck up a lively tune, and couples flooded the dance floor.

Raven searched the room, and not seeing the dark hair and broad shoulders she wished to see, headed to the refreshment table. Delightful, handmade fairies with iridescent wings and peach skirts perched on the edge of a bowl of persimmon pudding, pirouetted past piles of luscious fig tarts topped with gooseberries, and blew kisses by a platter of iced biscuits. Raven poured herself a glass of cranberry punch as Martha approached with a wide smile.

"I think this is quite the best turnout we've had yet, don't you?" Martha said, gesturing to the crush of people.

"Yes. I do think Mr. Scrooge would be pleased."

"When is the big announcement?" Martha asked.

"I am not..." Raven bit her lip, her optimism from moments before dashed. "...certain."

Martha searched her younger sister's face. "Uncertain when or...if?"

"I don't believe I have a choice if I wish for our family to remain in good standing." Raven felt a knot begin to form in her gut.

"We are hardly a traditional family. I think we will survive." Martha's sincere brown eyes held Raven's.

"But Mother wants—"

"Mother wants her children healthy and happy above all else." Martha gave an encouraging nod and then her eyes darted past Raven's head. "And here comes your solution now."

Raven turned to find Brit cutting through the crowd and the knot in her gut loosened, her muscles relaxing. And it wasn't because of the way he filled out his suit or the strong bones of his face. Or even the way he strode toward her with singular intent, eyes fierce, jaw flexing. It was that she now saw his huge, heart, his sharp mind, and his warrior's soul—as if he would fight any monster, overcome any obstacle to help those he loved, and even those he barely knew who needed him. Like little Joey.

The smile dawned from somewhere deep as she met his eyes.

He bent in a bow and extended his gloved hand. "How are you this evening, Miss Cratchit?" Then he arched a brow. "Or should I say Doc Cratchit?"

Impossibly, her smile widened. "I do love the ring of that title. But Raven will do...for you."

The long dimple appeared in his cheek as his lips tilted and he reeled her closer, his fingers brushing the bare skin of her arm below her sleeve and above the long glove she wore. "Well then, Raven," his voice a deep rumble. "Would you like to dance?"

"Yes," she answered in a breathless whisper.

They joined the waltzing couples and he asked, "So why a ball in an old warehouse? What is the significance of the name Fezziwig?"

Brit surprised her with the casual grace and the strength with which he moved her around the floor, so it took her a moment to catch her breath and respond, "Oh, Fezziwig is a nod to Mr. Scrooge's past."

Brit froze, and they stopped dancing mid-stride. "Did you say Scrooge?"

"Why yes. Ebenezer Scrooge. Did you know him?"

"It couldn't possibly be the same old curmudgeon," Brit said almost to himself.

"It most definitely could," Raven chuckled, remembering the miserly man Mr. Scrooge had once been. Before that long ago Christmas. Before three miraculous visitations that had opened his eyes to the true meaning of Christmas and, in turn, life.

As if he hadn't heard her, Brit said, "Because that man threw me out on my ear on Christmas Eve for spilling his precious stew."

Realizing they were blocking part of the dance floor, Raven drew Brit into a shadowed alcove behind a scarlet curtain and gazed up at his stunned countenance. "What do you mean?"

"I'd lived with traveling merchants for as long as I could remember, but that winter, the woman I'd believed to be my mother sold me to a crotchety old businessman. I worked for Scrooge for two weeks, and they were some of the most miserable days of my life." Brit raked his fingers through his hair, the strands gilded by moonlight streaming through a high window. "Or so I'd thought until I ended up living in the streets."

He looked like a lost, little boy as he stared into the middle distance, unblinking. Raven took his hand in hers. "You became a thief to survive."

"Yes." His heated gaze shifted to hers, brows lowered. "I blamed him...have *hated* Ebenezer Scrooge most of my life. How could he possibly be a hero to your family?"

Raven thought her heart might fracture for the young, abandoned boy Brit had been. She could see him; all long limbs, too-big feet, and freckles. She could see why he hated the man Ebenezer used to be. Brit glared into the middle distance as if reliving his past. She placed a hand on his arm. "I'm so sorry, Brit, for all you've endured. But believe me when I tell you that it is possible for people to change. Mr. Scrooge transformed into a generous, loving man who spent the remainder of his life helping others. Although that doesn't change what you endured because of him, I hope you can forgive him someday."

Brit's dark gaze moved back to hers and softened. "I cannot fully blame him. He was only one of a sequence of tragedies that shaped my life." He took a step closer to her. "Ultimately, it all led me to this moment. To you."

His singular focus upon her, Raven felt a blush heat her face.

"I wanted to thank you," he said.

"For what?" Raven lifted her eyes higher to meet his. Standing so close to him, she was hyperaware of his every move, his every breath.

"For everything," Brit replied, his voice low and soft as his hand moved up her arm.

"Why do I feel like this is a goodbye?" Raven whispered.

Brit's palm cupped her cheek, angling her chin with exquisite gentleness as his gaze locked on her mouth. His eyes churned like a starless sea, his hair tumbling across his brow as he whispered, "If it is, then I better make this count." He lowered his mouth to hers.

The kiss exploded through Raven like a firework. Brit's lips glided across hers, tender at first and then insistent as he wrapped his arm around her waist to lock her close. Raven melted into him. She had wanted this for so long, yet the touch of his lips, his tongue, exceeded all her expectations.

His big hands gripped her hips, and he deepened the kiss. Raven's world twisted and spun, merging into a fluid harmony that felt like molten heat and glorious fire in her veins. She caressed his neck, his jaw, his face, then her fingers slipped into the silk of his hair as she stood on her toes, straining to get closer. It was the sort of kiss that would imprint on her skin, her heart, forever.

He pulled back. "Bloomin' hell," he panted. "I'm sorry. That wasn't fair of me."

Raven, still catching her breath, but not willing to let him go, leaned her forehead against his chest. "Why are you saying good-bye?"

"Because after I lose the title, I doubt we will cross paths. An English proctor and a countess? You won't even visit Hill House as a doctor anymore."

She leaned back to look at him while keeping her arms around his waist. "First, who says I won't be doctoring? And more importantly, what do you mean lose the title?"

"I know John's wishes for your future, and I'm sorry for it." Gently, Brit removed her arms from around him and took a step back. "As to the rest, I thwarted John and George's plans to contest the will by destroying papers they had forged that disavowed my identity. But it wasn't enough. I mentioned to you that if I do not find a wife by my next birthday, I forfeit the title and the fortune. I suppose my father wanted to insure an heir. Which I understand, but that doesn't change the fact that my birthday is…tomorrow."

His dark gaze drilled into hers. "And there is only one person I wish to marry, and she…" He swallowed, his throat bobbing before he clarified, "*You* are promised to my brother."

"I don't care." The words escaped Raven's lips before she'd realized what she was going to say. "I'm not scared anymore. I want this…us."

Brit searched her face, heartache shining in his eyes as he said roughly, "I can't do that to you. I love you too much."

Before she could respond, he turned and slipped between the curtains.

What the bloody *hell*, had he just done?

Brit moved across the dance floor through swirling skirts, strode across the room to the refreshment table, and downed a glass of punch in one gulp. Unsure if he should stay or leave, he wandered toward a set of Christmas trees flanking a doorway. Perhaps if he could escape from the crowds and the noise, he could re-center his thoughts.

He slipped past the trees into a long, empty corridor lined on both sides with closed doors. He leaned against the wall, resting his head against the cool plaster as he squeezed his eyes closed.

Had he just left Raven alone after kissing her until neither one of them could breathe? After telling her he *loved her*? He'd never been a coward, but he sure felt like one.

He sighed. He had to go back and talk to her.

Brit pushed off the wall but before he could take a step, a hand gripped his shoulder from behind. "It's over."

John.

Brit turned and shook off John's grip as George stepped through one of the doorways and gave Brit a tight nod.

"What's over?" Brit demanded. "Your dignity? That, I can believe."

"You thought destroying our paperwork would change things, but it turns out we didn't have to do a thing. You disqualified yourself." John smiled slowly, lips stretching over lots of teeth. "The thought that you could take my place as earl is ludicrous. A street rat, like you? You don't have an ounce of Mother's dignity and you certainly aren't the leader your father was. You've never been good enough and you just proved it."

"I saw you sneak off the dance floor with Miss Cratchit," George said. "When she emerged, her hair was disheveled, and her cheeks bright red."

Brit opened his mouth to defend Raven when something John said caught his attention. *You've never been good enough...* What had John said the first day they'd met? *If I would have known—* He'd been referring to their father, *Brit's* father who had gone off the deep end and ignored John and George after Brit had been taken. Alarm bells sounded in Brit's head.

He'd missed a vital detail, a clue to what had happened to him all those years ago to separate him from his family. But it couldn't be. No one was that devious at such a young age.

Except maybe his own brother.

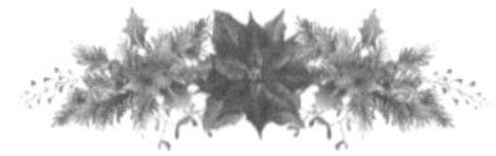

Raven walked to the table where she'd left her reticule and slumped into one of the fabric-covered chairs. Brit would lose everything...the title, the money, and his family's legacy if he didn't marry by midnight. She opened her handbag and checked the watch inside. It was after nine o'clock which meant he had less than three hours. Impossible.

But he loved her. Joy sparkled through her like bubbles of light. Each one of them popping as logic took over emotion. She would gladly marry him that night, but they couldn't marry by midnight without a license. *Pop.* She didn't care about his money or his title.

But clearly, he did. *Pop!* And she was already engaged to marry his brother. *POP!* She could break it off. She would do it right then before the wedding announcement was made.

She could still make this right.

Raven stood up and began to search the crowd. Surely, John and George had arrived.

"Raven," a voice spoke near her ear.

She spun to find Belinda *and* Archie Fox standing behind her.

Raven's hand flew to her chest. "You gave me a fright."

"I'm sorry," Bel said, "But there's something you need to see."

"Or hear," Archie said.

"Or both." Bel took her arm and it felt like a feather brushed across Raven's skin. "We have to go now." Bel led the way around the edge of the large room until they reached two Christmas trees disguising an opening. "Move in between the trees, and just listen," Bel whispered as if anyone else could hear her voice.

Raven searched her sister's hazy eyes for a moment and then quietly slipped between the branches of the trees and stopped when she heard a heated conversation happening down the corridor.

"What do you mean? How long have you presumed that you were the better heir to my father's legacy?"

That was Brit's voice and he sounded angry. Raven peeked through the trees in time to see John throw back his head and laugh raucously.

"How long?" John asked shaking his head. "Since the day you were born, Father stopped looking at me as his son. Stopped looking at me at all. It was all *you* and your black curls and angelic smile. The earldom had been promised to me! For eight years, Father had treated me like an equal. Trained me in estate management, taught me how to negotiate, how to be a good financial steward. He was grooming me to step into his role, but you stole it all just by being born!" John spat the words in Brit's face.

Brit glared back at him eye to eye, silence falling, heavy with implication. Then, almost as if pushed, Brit stumbled back two steps, his voice like ice. "What did you do, John?"

John glanced at his pocket watch and looked up with an evil grin. "It doesn't matter now. Your time is almost up, and you failed to marry. It's over Brit. You can go back to being a humble English teacher while I keep the mantle I was born to wear. I've won the title and the girl."

Raven's hands clenched into fists and her muscles tensed, but before she could come out of hiding, a soft voice whispered, "Wait."

His face set like stone, Brit leaned forward. "You're right, John. It is too late. I have no power to seek vengeance, so tell me the truth. You owe me that, at least."

"Fine. If it will help you sleep at night." John rolled his eyes to the ceiling. "You were a toddler and Father bade me watch you while he met with the town magistrate. We were sitting on the fountain in the square when I saw my opportunity. An old woman begged me for money. I gave her a coin and watched her hobble back to a painted wagon train. The idea hit me like lightning—the answer to all my prayers. I followed her and offered to pay her an exorbitant amount if she would meet me at the estate later than night and take you with them when they left town." John's eyes narrowed on Brit, and he said low, "I didn't much care what they did with you, as long as you never came back."

Even though Raven had suspected foul play had led to Brit's disappearance, she'd never expected that John had been involved. His diabolical plot stole the breath from her lungs.

Brit seemed to feel similarly as he gasped, "But you were only *twelve years old* at the time. How could you come up with something so..." he trailed off. "They could have killed me!"

"I told you, I didn't much care," John said blandly.

"John, that's enough," George warned his brother with a hand on his arm.

John chuckled. "It doesn't matter, George. We're in the clear. Brit is poor and powerless, and he can't prove a thing."

Raven couldn't take another moment and pushed out of her hiding place. "Perhaps with my testimony, he can."

All three men spun to face her.

"Raven..." John sputtered.

"I heard it all, John." She stalked forward. "That you had Brit kidnapped when he was a child! How could you? I knew you were cold, but this...this is evil!" Gripping her engagement ring, she jerked it off her finger and threw it with all her strength. The metal clattered at John's feet. "Consider our betrothal broken!"

John went pale and stared down at the glint of gold and gems on the floor before stooping to pick up the ring. He closed it in his fist and rose to his full height, his words measured, "Do you really think the magistrate will listen to the word of a former street thief and my disgraced castoff?"

"I spurned you, not the other way around," Raven said evenly.

John smirked. "Who would believe *you*, a base-born girl parading around as a doctor, would reject *me*, an esteemed peer of the realm? It's preposterous."

Without a word, Brit took three purposeful strides toward his brother, hauled back his arm, and punched John square in the nose.

John stumbled back, gripping his face as blood poured between his fingers.

Without hesitation, Brit followed and pummeled John in the stomach with one fist and then the other, making John groan and double over.

Raven, surprised by her own ruthlessness, thrilled at her ex-fiancé's comeuppance. The man deserved far more than fisticuffs, truth be told, but legal action would come later.

Brit leaned down and growled in John's ear. "Do not dare speak to her like that…" Brit reared back and hit his brother so hard on the chin that John fell like an axed tree, eyes rolling up in his head. "…ever again." Brit finished. Then he whirled on George, who made a squeak of fright before running down the hall and out a back door.

"Brit," Raven whispered and moved toward him. Brit's jaw flexed as his hands clenched and unclenched at his sides. She wanted to comfort him but did not think he would welcome it at that moment.

"Good on you, mate," Archie said cheerfully. "Wish I could've knocked out that blasted git myself."

Belinda appeared at Raven's side and put her arm around her shoulders. Raven was either in shock or her sister's touch felt less corporal than normal because Raven could see Bel's arm upon her but did not feel it.

Brit turned toward Raven, and when their eyes met his shoulders slumped, and she ran into his arms. "Brit, I'm so sorry. I hate what John has done and all he's taken from you. But I need you to know…" She leaned back to meet his eyes, her voice rough with emotion. "That I love you with all my heart, and I don't care a whit if you're an earl or a teacher or even a street thief. I want to be by your side always."

He searched her face. "Raven, I have nothing to give you. No way to provide the lifestyle you're accustomed to."

Archie cleared his throat behind them. "That might not be the case, old chap."

Brit arched an eyebrow at his old friend. "Out with it then."

"Archie and I." Bel stepped to Archie's side, and they linked hands, somehow appearing brighter and more vivid together. "With the help of a…er…friend, we have arranged a special marriage license that can be used tonight only."

Brit gently grasped Raven's upper arms and steered her toward him, his dark eyes flashing in the dim corridor. "I have no right to ask it of you, but if you meant what you said, I would be honored—"

"Yes, yes, yes! Of course, I'll marry you!" she exclaimed and threw her arms around his neck.

Brit hugged her so tight that he lifted her feet off the floor. "I love you, Raven Cratchit. I feel like I've waited my entire life to say that," he whispered in her ear. "So, if it's all right with you, I'm going to tell you every single day for the rest of our lives."

# Chapter Seventeen

*O*n that snowy night long ago, Brit took Archie's hand and together they made a way for themselves and others like them who had been discarded and abandoned. They plundered the streets of London town like a band of pirates taking back what should have been theirs.

*Thus began a remarkable friendship between two lost souls, a brotherhood more like, one that withstood time and testing.*

*And even death.*

St. George's church glowed with the soft flames of a massive chandelier, hundreds of candles lighting the gilded vault of the ceiling and reflecting in the multicolored stained-glass windows. Second-story galleries lined either side of the nave, walnut wood rails adorned with evergreen boughs and scarlet poinsettias.

Deep awe sparked in Brit's chest as he walked up the center aisle toward the ornate, gold cross. Who was he to have come so far? He'd gone from homeless orphan to marrying the woman of his dreams and inheriting the wealth and title of his noble father. It felt like too much goodness to hold, and he glanced back over his shoulder, half expecting Raven to have fled into the night.

But no, he saw her in the lobby surrounded by her family. Once the Cratchits heard the story of John's treachery, they had taken surprisingly little convincing to support Raven's decision to jilt John and marry Brit before midnight. The Cratchit family expected miracles, especially at Christmas, it would seem.

Brit inhaled the scents of melting wax and incense as he neared the dais when a hunched form stood from the pew to his right. Unkempt beard, a balding pate with stringy, gray hair to his shoulders. Brit sucked in a breath and stopped mid-stride. He knew this man. The Shadow from the orphanage who liked to hover near the back doors and dole out unsolicited wisdom. But before he could contemplate the man's presence, recognition sparked, and as if a veil had lifted from his eyes, Brit saw a thinner, more haggard version of the same person with eyes the gray of sleet, a beaked nose, and a hard, lipless mouth.

"Mr...Mr. Scrooge?" Brit managed to choke out.

The man hobbled forward and gave a nod. As he drew near, he seemed to grow and stretch, the pallor of his skin glowed, and the gray of his eyes shifted to glistening silver. Mr. Scrooge still appeared as Brit's old employer, yet with an ethereal cast.

And that's when Brit remembered that Raven had told him Mr. Scrooge was long dead.

Perhaps if Archie had not become Brit's constant companion after he'd passed, Brit would have run down the aisle screaming. But as the case may be, he only marveled at the old man's appearance. He did not seem to be a paler version of himself in life, as Archie did in his spirit form, but a fully metamorphosed transcendent being.

"It is I, my boy," Scrooge said warmly. "I am here not only to assist in the ceremony of your nuptials but to ask for your pardon. You came into my life before my miracle, you see, and I treated you mercilessly. Can you find it in your heart to forgive me?"

"I..." Brit was suddenly that lost boy again, discarded in the snow like rubbish. Those weeks after he'd been thrown out of Scrooge's basement had been the hardest of his life. If Arch hadn't come along when he had, Brit didn't like to think what would have happened to him.

But Archie *had* come along.

And so had Raven.

*Ebenezer Scrooge was quite a savior for our family.*

Just as Raven had saved him.

Brit felt suddenly lighter as he said, "I forgive you, Mr. Scrooge. I only regret that I did not have the privilege to know you after you found the light."

"Oh, you have." Mr. Scrooge laughed. "I've been hanging around for quite some time. Waiting for the right moment to reveal the Master's plan for your life."

"That's right. The old Shadow." Brit smiled bemusedly. "But what do you mean by plan?"

Scrooge glowed brighter as if the purity of his soul shown on the outside of his body. "The plan to prosper you and give you a hope and a future, of course," Scrooge said, his eager gaze shifting beyond Brit's shoulder. "Ahh...here we are now."

A cacophony of voices echoed behind him, and Brit turned to find at least twenty people filing into the nave; children with boots and coats thrown hastily over night clothes, all excited little faces that Brit knew well.

"Brit!" Chip Lightheart raced up the aisle, blond curls shining. "Are you really marrying Doc Cratchit?"

"And what if I am?" Brit grinned. If he were any happier, he might float into the rafters.

Chip's expression turned thoughtful. "I always did say you were the luckiest bloke I know."

"You might be right." Brit laughed as someone tugged on the hem of his jacket.

Brit looked down to see Joey's wide eyes staring up at him, his teddy bear clutched against his cheek. Brit knelt and picked the boy up, happy to feel a bit more meat on his bones. "I'm glad you came, Joey."

"Ain't it Christmas?" His freckled nose wrinkled in confusion as he glanced around. "Why are we in church?"

"Do you remember the story of the first Christmas that Olivia read last night?"

"About the baby in the manger and the angels?" He cocked his head and watched Brit's reaction.

"That's right, little chap." Brit kissed his rumpled head. "That's what we celebrate when we come to church at Christmas. But tonight is special because I'm also getting married."

Joey frowned.

"You'll understand someday," Brit said as he set the boy on his feet, and he scampered over to Chip as Jack and Olivia MacCarron approached.

Jack appeared stony faced as usual, while Olivia already had tears brimming in her golden-brown eyes as she said, "My brilliant boy, you did it. I am so happy for you."

Brit pulled Olivia into a one-armed hug. "How did you know to come?"

"We received a letter by courier from Mr. Bob Cratchit explaining that you and Raven had fallen in love," Jack said a bit gruffly. "The missive said that you planned to marry by midnight in order to claim your family's title and fortune, which I can understand." Jack's blue gaze locked on Brit's, and he understood that his mentor was not angry, but hurt. "What I don't understand, is why we knew nothing of this until now."

"He had to make his own way," Olivia said softly as she moved to Jack and looped her arm through his. "I remember a headstrong young scoundrel who did things his own way come hell or high water."

"Mrs. MacCarron!" Jack scolded, even as he grinned crookedly. "Cursing in church now, are we?"

Olivia lifted her pert little nose. "The good Lord knows I'm trying to make a point."

Jack kissed her cheek before turning to Brit. "I'm just grateful that Raven asked her father to contact us."

"I am as well. I'm afraid I've been a bit distracted." Brit shoved his hands in his pockets and shrugged.

Jack clasped his shoulder. "Completely understandable, my boy. You can tell us all about it when you are ready."

Brit nodded his thanks as frantic movements drew his attention to Archie waving at him from the front of the church. "I believe we are about to start," Brit said.

"Veck is here." Jack pointed to the bespectacled barrister seated unobtrusively in the back row. "He'll ensure everything is legal."

Brit gave a nod. For his parents, he would do everything within his power to continue their legacy and honor the earldom. The hint of trepidation for his new role must have shown on his face because Jack said softly, "You were always meant for more than leading a ragtag gang of orphans."

"Everyone could see it," Olivia confirmed.

Jack clasped Brit's shoulder and met his gaze. "I couldn't be prouder of you, if you were my flesh and blood son, Brit." Jack was a good man—one of the best—but not known for effusive sentiment. Which made the moment all the rarer and more precious. But Brit could not give in to the well of emotions that Jack's praise conjured.

Instead, Brit swallowed his tears and gave a single nod to Jack, before striding back up the aisle to where Archie waited for him in a shadowed recess.

"I'm standing up with you, mate. Even if the others can't see me, I'll be there." Archie's lopsided grin suggested the man he used to be before opium had stolen his life. He looked good and truly happy, if perhaps not as solid as before. In fact, Brit had to concentrate to bring his best friend into focus.

"I'm grateful for everything you've done, Arch. Are you the one who brought Mr. Scrooge into this?"

"The old Shadow?" Archie's gaze darted behind Brit, and Brit turned to see Ebenezer Scrooge wearing long, flowing robes, and holding a Bible.

Archie continued. "He's the one who gave me my second chance."

"Second chance at what?" Brit asked.

"It is time to begin. Please take your seats," Mr. Scrooge called, prompting everyone to move toward the front pews.

"Wait..." Brit stared. "They can see and hear him too? How is that possible?"

"Mr. Scrooge ain't like me and Bel," Archie said. "He already made amends for his wrongs in life. Now he helps other souls do the same."

Ebenezer Scrooge radiated light from the top of his bald head to the shining, gold slippers on his feet. "He's an angel," Brit breathed in awe.

"Something like that."

"Do the Cratchits recognize him?"

"Naw, not even Raven, I'm afraid. But that's for the best. He wouldn't want to upstage the bride and groom." Archie smiled and clapped Brit on the back (a gesture that felt like a soft breeze), and said, "Let's get you married!"

Brit couldn't feel his feet as he walked over and stood beside Mr. Scrooge. The narthex doors swung open to reveal Raven, wearing the same violet dress he'd seen her in earlier that evening, the jewels in her tiara glinting in the candlelight. But now, a lavender veil covered her face as she walked forward on her father's arm.

Perhaps he should feel doubts. They had decided to marry only hours before. But Brit had never felt more certain about any decision in his life. Securing the fortune and title was secondary to marrying the most incredible, kind, beautiful woman he'd ever known. The thought of waking up with her and spending every day at her side—making her happy and helping her change the world one person at a time—filled his chest to near bursting. All the love he'd missed out on as a boy had been returned to him and then some.

After Mr. Cratchit had given his permission for Brit to marry his daughter, Brit lifted the veil and gladly drowned in the lavender-blue sea of Raven's eyes as Mr. Scrooge spoke of keeping the delight of Christmas in every day. It was a beautiful speech and afterward, Brit and Raven exchanged the words and made the vows. Finally, Mr. Scrooge turned them to face the crowd.

"Now that Lord Brit Griffin and Raven Lucy Anne Cratchit have given themselves to each other by the promises they have exchanged before God and their loved ones, I pronounce them to be Lord and Lady Wexford, in the name of the Father, and of the Son, and of the Holy Spirit!"

Cheers and hoots rang out from the children, and the MacCarrons and the Cratchits applauded as the cathedral bells began to chime. This time, Brit didn't begrudge the gruff old bell marking the midnight hour. In fact, as the grand vibrations rang through the air, he thought it sounded less like teeth chattering in a frozen head, as he'd once thought, and more like joyous laughter from the heavens.

He took Raven's hand in his, and she stood on her toes to whisper, "I love you, Brit Griffin."

"And I, you," he replied into her ear, but when she gasped, he turned and followed her gaze.

At the far end of the aisle, another couple stood hand in hand in a near mirror image of themselves. Archie and Belinda, surrounded by incandescent light, began to rise into the air. All joyful smiles, Archie waved, and Bel blew a kiss just as their outlines faded and then flared brilliant white before winking out of sight.

Raven covered her mouth to muffle a sob.

Brit's eyes flooded until he could hardly see. Archie and Bel had both returned to atone for their wrongs and help the ones they loved most. Their lives on earth were finished. But they would spend eternity together.

Just like he and Raven.

Gently, Brit turned his wife to face him and smiled into her tear-filled eyes. It was Christmas Eve. A source of pain, not so long ago. Now rewritten as the happiest day of his life.

*The bell tolled twelve...*

# Epilogue

*O*ne Year Later
*Christmas Day*
*Wexford Manor in Hampshire*


Pristine snow coated the grounds of the estate. Raven gawked at the blanket of flakes sparkling in the rising sun like a million tiny diamonds. A world of white crystallized on every branch of the bare trees, the surface of the icy pond, and continued over snowy hills flowing into an azure sky.

Raven sighed with equal parts awe and contentment.

The peace felt well-earned after their whirlwind of a year. Brit had decided not to press legal charges against his brothers for arranging his kidnapping. He'd hired a new team of attorneys who had advised him against the long legal battle that would likely not turn out in his favor. They had no proof besides John's confession which he had officially retracted. Instead, Brit had disowned his brothers, thereby removing any chance of their future schemes to take back the earldom. Last they had heard, the scandal had chased

John and George out of London and they were currently living somewhere in Greece.

"Do you like it here, my love?" Brit asked as he wrapped her in his arms from behind.

This was Raven's first visit to the Hampshire estate. While Brit had educated himself on all the responsibilities and privileges of the title of earl, Raven had continued to grow her medical practice, even putting out a shingle on an office in London where she saw patients three days a week. It turned out women from all walks of life preferred a female physician, especially for the ailments that were unique to their sex. She still volunteered her services where she was needed and found that her new status as a countess stopped the tongues of the ton from wagging about it overly much. The formidable Countess Waldegrave took care of the rest of the aristocracy, resulting in far more social invitations than Brit and Raven had the inclination to accept.

Raven relaxed against Brit's broad frame, soaking in the warmth of his large body wrapped around hers. "Tis' magical," she said. "Like a Christmas wonderland all our own."

His lips lowered to the sensitive spot on the curve of her neck, and she felt his soft kisses in every nerve ending and cell of her body. This man had the power to turn her into the consistency of figgy pudding with a single touch. She turned in his arms to gaze at the face she loved most in the world and lifted on her toes to kiss his perfect mouth.

His lips pressed into hers, a silken brush. She clutched the hard muscles of his arms, sinking into his delicious heat as he slanted his mouth and deepened the kiss.

A thunderous noise broke them apart as dozens of feet tromped down the main staircase, jovial voices cascading over one another in excited cheer. The occupants of Hill House had been promised gifts and cake for breakfast. Jack and Olivia, and Mrs. March herded them into the dining room where a feast awaited. Presents would follow, then a gingerbread decorating contest and delivery of cookies to every tenant on the Wexford estate's two hundred acres.

"Perhaps not *all* our own," Brit said laughingly.

Raven touched her forehead to his. "Even better, Lord Wexford."

The title no longer spooked him, and Brit leaned down to kiss her again as a throat cleared behind them. They turned to find Bob Cratchit, arms crossed and wearing a stern scowl, defused by the twinkle in his eyes. "I will not protest to this public display if perhaps there is a grandchild in my near future." He lifted caterpillar brows in question.

"Not as yet, Father." Raven went to embrace him. "But you will be the first to know."

Martha, her husband and children in tow, appeared next. Followed by Peter and his new wife, then Matthew, and finally Tim who rubbed a hand over his wild hair and said, "I'm only up at this hour because I was promised cake."

Brit laughed and pointed toward the dining room.

Mrs. Cratchit emerged from around the corner, wearing a long apron, a dusting of flour on her plump cheek.

"Mother!" Raven flew over to her. "How long have you been awake?"

"Too long." She gave a tired smile. "But someone had to oversee our very first Christmas as a combined family!"

Raven knew it was no use arguing. "Let's go partake then, shall we?"

The day held all the chaos and joyful abandon that only children at Christmas could bring; gifts were exchanged, carols were sung, cookies made and delivered, followed by a rowdy snowball fight that left them all drenched and cold to the bone. Which made their gathering by the immense fireplace in the main parlor with everyone wrapped in robes and warm woolen socks while they sipped hot chocolate, all the more satisfying.

Raven curled up beside Brit on the sofa, their hands entwined, as they listened to her father's annual retelling of Ebenezer Scrooge and the three spirits of Christmas's past, present, and future. It was the first time Brit had heard the story, since on Christmas day the previous year, they had been a bit preoccupied.

As her father wove the tale, taming down some of the scarier moments, the children of Hill House ooh'ed and aah'ed at all the appropriate places. When he reached the ghost of Christmas future, Joey ran to Brit and curled up in his lap, clutching his teddy. Raven couldn't say that she blamed him—that silent, shadowed spirit had starred in many of her nightmares over the years.

"After that night," Mr. Cratchit went on. "Mr. Scrooge had no further interaction with spirits, good or ill. But it was said of him ever afterwards that he knew how to keep Christmas well, if any man alive possessed the knowledge. And so, we shall all hold Christmas in our hearts every day of the year!"

Everyone clapped, and Raven glanced over to see tears shimmering in Tim's eyes. Mr. Scrooge had not only saved his life but had been like a grandfather to him. They exchanged a knowing smile and Tim quickly blinked away his emotion, then rose with a grin to play his requisite role. "God bless us, every one!" he pronounced. "Now let's get some biscuits!"

The children cheered and followed Tim out of the room, including little Joey.

"They'll never sleep now," Olivia lamented and rested her head on Jack's shoulder.

"That is Tim's responsibility," Jack said as he stood with his sleeping daughter in his arms. The toddler woke at the sound of his voice and then snuggled in closer to his neck. Jack kissed her forehead as he extended his hand to help Olivia to her feet. The couple made married life appear so idyllic that Raven hoped she and Brit could maintain such a relationship over time.

Bit by bit, everyone left the room, leaving Raven and Brit alone in the glow of the candles on the tree, the only sound the soft crackle of the fire. As happy as Raven felt, her heart still longed for her sister.

"Do you think they're happy?" Raven asked quietly.

"Archie and Bel?" Brit inquired; his thoughts aligned with hers as usual. "I do."

"Sometimes, I miss her and then feel completely selfish for doing so."

Brit's arm tightened around her and when he responded his voice was thick with emotion. "I didn't know if I should tell you this, because well," he cleared his throat. "It's not an easy thing to hear, but Arch came to me right before our wedding and told me he'd been given a second chance to amend for his wrongs in life. That's why he hung around all those years after his passing."

Raven sat up and stared at him. "What?"

"Now that I've heard the story of Mr. Scrooge and understand a bit better, I feel all the more grateful that Archie, and perhaps Bel, did not have to wander the earth as broken spirits and were given the chance to spend eternity in heaven together," Brit said as he tenderly tucked a strand of hair behind Raven's ear, his warm hand lingering on her jaw.

Raven's vision blurred, her throat closing. "Bel was stuck here because of *me*?"

"It wasn't like that. She was granted a second chance." Brit brushed a thumb under her eye, catching her tears. "You found her, didn't you? When she died."

Raven nodded and closed her eyes against the image of her sister's dead body, her sightless eyes.

"I was the one who found Archie as well, and I blamed myself for years for not arriving soon enough to save him."

"I did too," Raven gasped.

Brit tugged Raven close, and she nestled against his warm throat, savoring the vibration of his voice as he said, "Here's what you need to understand, that I have just now come to realize about Archie. Bel's death was not your fault, Raven. She made a choice that led to her demise. They both took their lives into their own hands and stepped outside of God's will for them. Helping us find our happiness freed them from their guilt and allowed them to accept God's forgiveness so they could move into the light of eternity. They finally understood that we cannot save ourselves. Only God can do that. All we have to do is accept the gift He offers."

"The ultimate gift of Christmas," Raven breathed.

"I think Mr. Scrooge would approve of that assessment."

Raven snuggled against Brit's warmth and realized a weight had lifted from her heart. She felt light and fizzy like anything was possible. She was exactly where she was meant to be, and so was Bel. They would reunite someday. But as she lifted her face to Brit's for a kiss, she hoped not too soon.

"Happy Christmas, love," Brit murmured and kissed all of Raven's melancholy thoughts away.

# Olivia Twist

**TO READ JACK AND OLIVIA'S STORY, CHECK OUT OLIVIA TWIST!**

Praise for OLIVIA TWIST...

"Delectable romance, spine-tingling danger, and an indomitable female lead make Lorie Langdon's *Olivia Twist* an addictively exquisite romp. One that kept me up far past midnight!"
—MARY WEBER, author of the Storm Siren Trilogy

"Langdon has crafted a charming reimaging of the classic story *Oliver Twist*. There is a perfect balance between historical details, solid pacing, and strong character voices. Readers may find this book to be a bit more hopeful than the original story by Charles Dickens, but the plight of the poor in London in the 1800s is still apparent. It is easy to root for the characters, particularly the intelligent and kick-butt heroine, Olivia. If you are looking for a historical tale full of adventure, twists, and a bit of romance, this is one to check out."

—ROMANTIC TIMES

"Captivating from the very first page to the very last! *Olivia Twist* is an enchanting story, brimming with eclectic characters, intrigue, and a romance that is certain to leave you weak at the knees. Not to be missed!"

—JEN TURANO, USA Today Best-Selling Author

# Discussion Questions:

1. Do you believe in spirits? Have you ever seen or witnessed evidence of a ghost?

2. Raven fought the conventions of society to follow her calling as a female doctor. Have you ever gone against popular opinion to fight for something you believed in?

3. Brit lived on the streets as an orphan pickpocket. He had always been an aristocrat but had a hard time overcoming who he thought he was to step into his birthright. Have you overcome challenges from your past to become the person you are today? If so, how have you successfully altered your perception of yourself?

4. In Dickens's *A Christmas Carol*, Ebenezer Scrooge's transformative experience turns his life around. In a more subtle shift, Brit also changes for the better, letting go of his anger and his past to carve a new path for his life. Do you believe other people can truly change? Give an

example.

5. What is the true meaning of Christmas to you?

# About the Author

Lorie Langdon is the author of the international Disney Villain series, Happily Never After, featuring legendary villains such as; Ursula Vanessa, Gaston, Yzma, Captain Hook, and the Evil Queen. Each book is a glimpse into the villains' origins and their experiences of first love. Her short story ANNA and THE KING can be found in the Frozen anthology, All is Found.

Lorie is also an Amazon best-selling author of YA novels; the DOON Series, GILT HOLLOW, and OLIVIA TWIST, which was picked up by Target Stores across the nation and is contracted for film by Lonetree Entertainment. She is an international speaker who has been featured on such media as; USAToday, NPR Radio, EntertainmentWeekly, RedbookMagazine, and Girl's Life Magazine.

When she's not writing, Lorie is an avid bookstore explorer and enjoys traveling with her husband and two sons.

www.ingramcontent.com/pod-product-compliance
Lightning Source LLC
Chambersburg PA
CBHW061809190726
48289CB00007B/2132